Ovidiu Slavoiu

MANA

Inspired by Soka, my day-to-day motivation.
Encouraged by Pooja, my link to reality.

Contents

Acknowledgments

This book is an entrepreneurial project. It's a pursuit to prove my vocation and to answer several personal questions. It's also an older dream.

Along the way, I was lucky to meet wonderful, generous people who offered their support, time, energy, openness, creativity, ideas, advice, confidence, enthusiasm, appreciation, passion, empathy, curiosity, criticism, questions, solutions…all those ingredients a dreamer needs in order to take the next step.

They are all "normal" people. **MANA** couldn't have reached this point without their help. I looked for "normal" readers' feedback and blessing. Because readers are the most credible critics.

At the same time executioners and victims, my closest collaborators were my wife Carmen, and one of my best friends, Puiu "Explorish" Hertioga. They were probably the most persistent and merciless critics of my work. Carmen (or Pooja as I call her at home) has also taken the author picture on the back cover. Puiu has constantly challenged me along the whole project: the plot, the storyline, the pace, the first paragraph of the book (!), the title, the colors of the cover, the publishing option, the marketing stuff, going in print or going e-book… all in all, the very best coach.

Wilhelm Salater (aka Victor Alartes), an author himself, gave me his blessing on the plot line and on the clarity of depicting the main character. Rodica Guja and her editorial experience confirmed me that the book is by no means cursory, but generous enough ("Maybe too generous, as you open too many doors"); and original in many respects. Eventually she passed MANA over to Feri Balin (also a SF author), who asked me frankly: "Ovidiu, why do you have doubts?" Both Rodica and Feri brought me the confidence I needed to move on.

Victor Rosu was probably the fastest reader of my draft: ONE afternoon! He opened my eyes on the Spinozan path of the story. Another good friend of mine, Ciprian Paltineanu, probably as fast as Victor, brought in the "technical" consistency (martial arts related) to one of my action passage; and, thus, sorted out a plot dilemma.

Dan Radulescu, a heavy reader, challenged me to change the initial title. I have partially redesigned the first part thanks to my younger colleague, Vlad Sabau. I have also "tamed" the language of the book (a little bit hermetic at version 20; the last version is 33...), thanks to another younger colleague, Cosmin Buteica.

My aunt-in-law, Irina Popa, a wonderful lady, is the daring translator of my book. She passed the translation further to another generous gentleman, Dean Hufstetler, who has given the translation the very eye of an English native. Thank you Irina, thank you Dean!

The cover picture is Sorin Onisor's creation. When I first saw it, I said: "This photo best suits my climactic point!". Thank you Sorin for your openness and support! Eventually, my good friend, Alex "Mason" Podoleanu has architected the cover with its simple, elegant design.

My decision to go self-publish was strengthened by my former college colleague, Simona David, an author herself.

There were also several other curious reviewers: my mother Marioara Slavoiu, Gordon Clark, Lacramioara Isarescu, Razvan Toma, Adrian Visinescu, Stefan (the father) and Alex (the son) Pais who gave me their feedback and the "readers' blessing".

Last, but not least, I want to thank Adina Cretu, the one who structured the elegant and friendly design of the book website: www.budofcore.com.

Thank you all, again!

Now… let's start the quest!

Part One

VOCATION

A perfection of means and a confusion of goals;
these seem to be our main issues.
Albert Einstein

Imbalance

(The Core had again felt distortions in the Flow. This was different from what it had experienced before. Therefore it had to understand the cause of these new fissures.

The first contact it had initiated with the Carriers had been engendered by an evolution. At the time, the Core helped them become more than instinctual creatures.

The second incursion had been occasioned by degradation in the quality of the Flow. Then the Core had decided to inspire a Speaker, both to determine the cause and to fix the ruptures. And even though through that mission the Speaker had changed the lives of the Carriers forever, he had had to pay a very high price. And despite his good teachings, their interpretations were subsequently wrong, either willingly or by mistake, and that was how those teachings were passed on.

Maybe that was why there followed a long period of stagnation.

The Core had to continue to polish those teachings. It was to initiate, then, for the third time, an incursion in the existence of the Carriers, this time, though, not through speaking emissaries, nor by inspiring the Carriers…this time, the incursion had to be through direct contact.

The Core only had to find the right Carrier.)

The Ritual

She woke up at daybreak again. Her agitated sleep was getting ever more annoying. No, the agitation wasn't from dreams...rather, it was awake slumber. Night after night the same: she could neither rest nor rise from her bed because of those clusters of lights and shadows that the eyes of her mind saw. For a good few months, she had spent her nights prey to those bizarre feelings, when she seemed to be travelling the universe from one end to the other, searching for the Holy Grail of her own peace of mind. She seemed to be in search of either a damned, imprisoned, homeless soul or of a blessed and liberated one.

Each time she woke, she felt that she was sinking deep into her large bed, three square meters. Three square meters where she, a small and slender being, was lost...the bed was too large, half-empty, and cold.

Something in her wouldn't rest. It was getting frustrating. She often wondered how long she could last at that pace. And during all this time, her mind worked on.

It's like I'm a zombie...Is it a sign? Is there something wrong with my head, or is it just dissatisfaction? Have I neglected anything? Brutal revenge...

(Sleep, dear girl, sleep.)

Was she yearning for affection? She, Yuzuki Tanaka? Since when?

Although physically she felt exhausted, paradoxically, her intellect felt more fresh and thirsty than ever. What most intrigued her was this condition, partly illusive, that also occurred during the day. Not once did she realize she had missed the sense of the talks with her fellow professors or with the students during the breaks of the colloquies she delivered at the Department of Applied Psycho-sociology at the State University of Moscow.

The famous Lomonosov University had been her choice for the follow-up of her PhD, which she had started back home in Kanazawa, at JAIST.[1] Perhaps that was the reason for her sleeplessness; her project was moving slowly. Or maybe her interrupted sleep was due to that large, half-empty bed. Or maybe she was just worrying over nothing.

That's how it is when you know too much about how your head works...

And yet, that jumpy sleep and the dreams, without a beginning or an end, "speaking" about nothing, had become a burden, a host of feelings that left her with too

[1] Japan Advanced Institute of Science and Technology

many unfinished thoughts. Paradoxically, many of them seemed to provide inspiration.

Will I be forever alone?

She dreamed of a family. She wanted a child, but it took two for that.

"If you want to win, you've got to play."

That was how her friend Orrin had teased her, offering, half-jokingly, half seriously, to help her when she was finishing her second master's degree at Harvard.

"If you want a baby, I could help…"

"You Americans, how you seem to think you can solve everything…"

Yuzuki was dreaming of a love story, but a true one. It was one of the refuges in her moments of awakened loneliness, where refuges were otherwise few and short-lived. She felt that her soul had been left behind somewhere in her teenage years, when any meaningful smile of a boy had unsettled her for a day and a night. But only that long. She soon returned to her own time…and the boys, grown men now, smiled less and less often at her. Not that they didn't want to, but they didn't have anyone to whom they wanted to give their smiles. And if it did happen today, most of the time, she missed those windows of opportunity. She felt too smart for many of them, and she tried to show that systematically.

She suddenly sat up, still dizzy with sleep. She crawled to the carefully furnished kitchen, almost unused in the past two years since she had arrived in Moscow. She couldn't cook because she didn't particularly like to eat. It seemed a waste of time.

But she loved coffee!

Eyes half-open, she put the *Nespresso* tablet into the machine and pressed the small, red, magical button. She gave a satisfied sigh. The machine purred discreetly, like a cat that had been scratched between its ears. Then came the powerful, unique smell, rising from the droplets of bitter sap dripping from the machine…and life began to make sense.

Still half-asleep, she took the first sip of the creamy hot liquid. She felt herself coming to life, all her fears gone, her troubled sleep held back in her big, cold, empty bed. She leaned against the door of the cabinet masking the fridge, eyes partially closed turned to the dim light of the Moscow spring morning. Then she came to understand the assertion of a colleague who, at a conference on social behavior, had said that people didn't drink their coffee for the taste or for the smell, but for the ritual; it was everyone's entrance into daytime, unique and personal. She was just going through her ritual. The first coffee of the day was divine. And if anyone dared interrupt that moment…there was nobody.

On the way to the bathroom, she began to mentally program what she had to do. She checked her agenda during her long shower: what she had to say at the first seminar, what meetings she had, what she knew about the people she was to meet. While she was drying her hair, she got a glimpse of herself in the mirror…a beautiful, intelligent face, but absent and tired, judging by the discreet rings under her eyes, which were slightly swollen—a face caught under the mask of full intellectual focus, which was written in every grimace, pore, and wrinkle.

Creation...her meaning. Her destiny. She had turned thirty, and often she felt that her life had gone by like a *maglev*, stimulated only by her contagious passion for work.

Six and a bit. Early...the university opened at 7:30 a.m., and her apartment was only ten minutes' walk away. It was a big, spacious apartment with high ceilings, located in the building reserved for various protocol services and for professors who came on short-term assignments to Lomonosov—different guests, lecturers like herself, arriving from different parts of Russia or elsewhere on the globe. The building was austere on the outside; it had been built during the Soviet era and had, just like the university's "temple," a sober and authoritarian look. It was guarded discreetly, but well.

On the inside, things looked quite different. The rooms were modern and cozy sometimes, even though minimalist. The classic aura was still retained in the heavy wooden furniture, candelabra, and wall paneling, either silky and beautifully embroidered or wooden, carved with Russian folk elements. Paintings of Russian life complemented the atmosphere in the rooms and hallways. You could "read" a good part of the unwritten Russian history just by walking around in the building.

In the apartment itself, everything was grand and welcoming —the doors, the bedroom, the living room where Yuzuki had arranged her den, the bathroom, the bathtub, the kitchen. Initially she had regarded the apartment as a waste of space and resources. She was used to the small spaces, used to their fullest, of her native Japan. Later she had gotten used to her new house, and often she thought that once back in Kanazawa, she would feel unfamiliar and cramped.

She felt best in the living room. The walnut bookcase covered a whole wall, around four meters long and three meters high. The doors to the balcony, the only smaller space, were in this room; from here she would often watch the huge university building and the park surrounding it.

Near the balcony door, opposite the bookcase, Yuzuki had ordered a large table where she kept all her tools: computers, printer, scanner, notes, studies, and reports. Many colored pencils and markers. Behind the desk, a big plastic board still showing random ideas…all was orderly, though. Organized. Disciplined.

Her lecture was to begin at eight. Until then…time for a good hunk of work.

The Salmon

She brewed a second coffee and activated her "Salmon."

With one touch of the keyboard pad, Yuzuki thawed the three big white monitors on which she watched the state and feelings of humankind in the virtual world, 24/7. The Salmon were the core of her PhD thesis. With the help of the algorithms behind them, she tried to anticipate the spontaneous reactions of the different types of network "prosumers."

The clue to her work was the meeting of two worlds, information technology and applied psychology, and once the two merged, the permanent discovery of new patterns of collective thinking. She used technology to decipher the sense of some words or key terms used by the large numbers of users on the several sources she surveyed.

The goal was to create a simple tool, handy for the users of the Salmon, through which people could obtain, quickly and relevantly for their areas of interest, content summaries for various fields of activity such as economics, business, politics, or sociology. In theory, any topic or field of interest could be investigated to delineate trends connected to the evolution of that particular field, with an assumed error margin, of course. The number of sources she surveyed had multiplied in time; they would have looked overwhelming to the common user who dared look at the three monitors. On top, the sources were in different languages. The Salmon probed in real time all these targeted sources.

Yuzuki had thought to make the lives of Salmon users easier, so she had designed filters that could dynamically change the hypotheses of the searches by alternating combinations of key terms and notions or by defining multiple goals for those "probes" and analyses.

For her thesis, she had selected a few pilot fields that had seemed controversial enough, since she needed a critical, credible base to calibrate her algorithms. These fields were global financial reform, the Middle East situation, a few small, isolated cases of political tensions in emerging countries, and, of course, the effects of information technology on social dynamics. She had added the last one because her Salmon depended a lot on the direction of information technology. Like any other person proposing a daring idea, she had encountered criticism and skepticism.

"The thesis regarding the network users' autonomy of thinking is as relevant as that of a box office success movie: it is attractive, but temporary. People no longer think with their brains; therefore, Miss Tanaka's product, although incorporating a great amount of work and laudable for its goal, hypotheses, and areas of applicability, will change nothing of our limited capacity, as a civilization, of preventing ample economic and social crises. This is due to one simple motive: 'free will' is a stillborn concept. Mankind was, and is, 'guided' by those who, randomly or purposefully, decide that things must go in one particular direction."

Yuzuki had been devastated for two days, all the more since the comment had come from a Japanese sociologist. The Salmon were just tools used to validate the "network democracy;" that was all!

Why this confusion with autonomy? Did I ever say that I wanted to stop crises? Some people just pour out their frustration on other people's work without even understanding what it is all about. ».

She admitted that here and there, the general feeling of the networks might have a purposeful character and that many times, people are influenced by illegitimate leaders of opinion. But that was a different story. She truly believed, despite this, that the reactions of a large community could still be spontaneous and beyond control, influence, and manipulation.

The ironies had continued from the critics:

"Undoubtedly, Asimov is one of the most intuitive and influential fiction writers in the history of mankind, but the ideas of the Foundation saga are still science fiction. It was to be expected that someday a daring researcher would try to give a palpable dimension to Asimov's psychohistory. Yet it is hard to walk in the footsteps of such a titan, especially since he saw this development as taking place millennia from now. Yuzuki Tanaka thinks it can be done within a decade. We wish her luck."

Yuzuki had been granted a reply:

"History is not short of skeptics. Nor is it short of dreamers...great dreams or not. The skeptics forget, though, perhaps too often, about one half of 'SF'—the 'S,' which is exactly the one that must be transposed into practice to the level accessible to the technology and the maturity of humankind at a given moment. Humans reached the moon after a Jules Verne script, and although the author had many lapses, the idea was finally achieved. Yes, maybe I am a daydreamer. But why couldn't psychohistory or its first buds begin with studying the feelings and reactions of networks?"

Once she had tried a case study, starting from the fact that the investors in financial markets accept the idea that by understanding the feelings and the emotions of people in virtual space and by cleverly modeling their trends, one can come to anticipate the evolution of equities and other securities on global markets. She had offered the example of that partial but successful application of her solution to a Japanese investment fund, which, based on the analysis of comments in the Japanese blogosphere and on the social networks used by Japanese players, was able to anticipate the trend of that particular fund pretty accurately. A specialized site had questioned:

"Perhaps it was just the ability of that fund's manager. The correlation with the market feeling came only as confirmation. Can you determine a causal link between the two?"

Yuzuki had explained that the whole line of reasoning was based on the algorithms of her Salmon. She had not been too convincing...and she was certain they hadn't even tried very hard to understand.

Then an investor came who had understood the potential of the Salmon and who had offered Yuzuki the much-needed financing, on condition that in two years at the latest, the company that was to be built as a special purpose vehicle around the Salmon would be listed on the stock exchange. Yuzuki had declined the offer.

"This tool cannot itself be subjected to perception; it is a tool that anyone interested can use if he or she wants to understand certain social dynamics. Consequently, it must stay objective, neutral. It is a logical conflict to take something like that onto the market... besides, I cannot guarantee that I will finalize all checkpoints and all validation tests of the system within two years."

They had explained that she could launch a stable but still preliminary version at first. Then many other new versions could be implemented...and she could divide the Salmon into several complementary product categories. She had stayed with her initial proposition. She received no further sign from them. And of course, no financing.

Jackals…

She had remained confident and focused on her idea. Therefore, she was not surprised to read the following:

"In parallel with official statistics, central banks have started to watch a novel economic indicator by analyzing people's searches on Google in order to determine the evolution of demand."

Others had also thought how to exploit "the wisdom of crowds." It was only normal. And she expected that sooner or later, other ideas similar to her Salmon would turn up. Only sometimes she felt like Quixote.

Am I too arrogant? Or too romantic? Or simply naive… What if they're right?

She had been asked by a journalist why "Salmon." To which she had replied:

"Because they are special fish, capable of living both in salt and in fresh water. Because they are the symbols of wisdom. They have a spirit of adventure and sacrifice unique to the fish and not only the fish, being capable of swimming against the current for thousands of miles to spawn. They are a key factor for many ecosystems. They simply inspire me, so I chose that the spirit of their life be mirrored in my creation. It is just a metaphor, nothing too elaborate…"

Each time, she turned back to the *Bushido* spirit. Meditation helped her get over her frustrations.

She had started thinking about the Salmon while still an undergraduate. And now, almost a decade later, the Salmon were almost ready to swim through the sources of information. If only for this, she had to go on.

Like she had dreamed.

I.

Tiredness prowled around. She felt her eyelids drooping, but her mind would not find its natural refuge.

I am daydreaming again…

She gradually slipped into slumber. Only something was different. She felt herself rising above the things around her, as if sucked up by an unseen force, bathed in a kind of phosphorescent light. Then a vibration, ever stronger; then…

Nothingness enveloped her. She felt none of the familiar sensations. Total darkness. Perfectly quiet. She seemed to be floating in a dimensionless void, a moldable space that sensed her every thought, her every imagined movement. Coming down somehow, as if regular orientation made any sense, a warm, welcoming light approached. Yuzuki could make out a few silhouettes. Two, then three, then seven, then three again… then suddenly they multiplied, and she lost count. Upon a closer look, they seemed to have wings…

Angels? What beautiful angels…

She put her imaginary hand out and noticed that her own silhouette was shrouded in a cold, white light, like transparent silk fluttering in an invisible wind.

Who are you?

The perfect faces gave no answer. They only smiled and went away. She wanted to follow them, but she realized that the same current that had brought her there was now taking her back.

The same vibration, the same light, the same feeling of imponderability. She woke up with a start, tears in her eyes.

A sense of infinite happiness embraced her consciousness. The room was bathed in light. But this was the light of a warm spring sun.

The Friend

Yuzuki had adapted to life in Moscow, despite her initial reserve. Many of the walls she had built and the prejudices she had fuelled against "Mother Russia" and its people had vanished, one by one. Gradually, she even came to admire them. She had read a good part of Russia's classic literature and had seen many ballet performances. She began to understand the language, so she even tried theater a few times.

Orrin Hammet, her American friend who had offered to "help" her make a baby, had visited her in Moscow within six months of her move to Lomonosov. She told him enthusiastically what she had discovered since her arrival.

"You'll get over it. And yet…from where is this respect for these numb brutes of the East?"

"Orry, for us, they are the West…*you* are the East."

"Yuzuki, get real."

"You're brainwashed, Orry. You are. You too have had major social cramps, almost all the time. What makes you think that Russia does not learn from its own mistakes? It is quite risky to judge a people without considering its cultural landmarks. And damn superficial to consider that you can wipe out a whole absurd century in only a few short years."

"Each nation has the destiny it deserves…"

"*What?* So you say that the Enola Gay's promenade over Hiroshima was legitimate? Or you think that the ordinary Japanese gloated over the "carnival" of Pearl Harbor?"

"It's not the same."

"It's not the same... History is not always written by people with a vision. What should be the landmark? What should demonstrate the superiority of one people, according to your superior Yankee mind? Or, er...its spiritual maturity?"

"Now you're going to tell me that our social system is idiotic and anachronistic."

"It isn't idiotic, Orrin. But it could become anachronistic shortly. Yes, you are the *de facto* creators of efficient management and structural mechanisms. But don't forget; nothing lasts forever, especially empires. And watch out, bad news! You no longer are a model of morality and good faith. Many 'numb brutes' on this earth have started to understand how things really stand with Uncle Sam. He is as weird as Santa Claus riding in a Coca Cola sleigh."

"The whole globe speaks our language," Orrin bragged like a child. "Even you teach in English here in Moscow. What about that?"

"For now. And if only it was your language. Do you have an idea how high the interest in the Mandarin language has risen in the last three years? Four hundred percent!"

"China, more delayed fireworks...see the sparks when it fires!"

"You're lost!"

They went back to their own memories. Yuzuki had met Orrin while getting her master's degree at Harvard.

They had worked together on their final dissertation. As it was somewhat fashionable, they had concentrated on the impact of technology on social dynamics and the human psyche. Orrin had covered the areas concerning identity and individual autonomy, while Yuzuki dealt with the sociology part—phenomena and manifestations like co-creation, crowdsourcing, crowd-funding, and prosumerism. Somehow, that had included all collective associations determined in one way or another by the explosion of technology within various "tribes." The two of them had reached the conclusion that yes, technology increases individual autonomy and fundamentally alters the notion of "average" and that by technology, certain communities "burn" stages of development.

Their conclusion:

"Technology acts at the topmost level of Maslow's pyramid. Through technology, we acquire more self-control and self-confidence, which, paradoxically, makes us less dependent on the community."

And the *motto*...

"Self-control—the only solution to survive in a world dominated by idiots."[2]

That had amused the evaluation committee, and Yuzuki and Orrin had been awarded a good grade. Later, Orry got a lecturer position at the Anthropology Department

---

[2] *DeMotivation*, http://www.demotivation.us/self-control-1245173.html

at Berkeley, California. He had begun his PhD, somewhat emboldened by Yuzuki's ambition. His subject had to do with human cloning because, for him at least, it was a controversial issue. During Orrin's visit, he and Yuzuki had discussed about it over dinner in her Moscow apartment.

"So, Orry…tell me about your work."

"My work…when you say that, I already see an idol surrounded by flowers and torches."

"I knew you as an erudite, profound guy."

"What kind of profoundness are you talking about: Hungarian, Romanian, or Jewish?"

"Come on, nobody's perfect; so stop complaining and tell me!"

"Seeing that the cloning subject feels like arguing, I started from a threat hypothesis. It was only natural to approach it emotionally, right? I thought it might be useful to draw attention, sociologically speaking, to the fact that by cloning, one might arrive at an identity crisis. Our dear autonomy! My idea is connected to the 'totem' of genetic individuality. Life is a universal privilege that, morally, not to mention from a religious point of view, we have the obligation to respect. And since we challenge the creation of life anyway, we should at least make sure we don't get destroyed in the process."

Yuzuki tried to appear objective and to keep focused. Many of the things she heard from Orrin had been the subject of their debates several times before.

"Then…human cloning is considered late and forced in the cell development, which apparently leads to a partial loss of the genetic characteristics of the predecessors. The mother egg and the father seed would not have thought at the moment of their miraculous meeting that a silly syringe would tease their nuclear 'romance'…"

"Orry, sorry for the interruption, but would you like some more wine?"

Despite her emancipation, Yuzuki still kept something of the Japanese woman's behavior, where a woman organically felt the need to serve the man in front of her.

"Yes, please. Of course, for the moment, the debate refers to certain special situations. Either the parents want another child and cannot have it for various reasons, but they would still want their own child, or, worse, their child died or had an accident…and they want their child back. They collect genetic material from the first child and they 'make' the second one. Nothing to reject; I may accept that their wish is legitimate. Emotionally…humanely…"

Orrin had closed his eyes and continued, his face to the ceiling. Yuzuki was fascinated by the passion he displayed in his dialogues.

"Still, the problem remains. Whether we like it or not, this issue goes beyond the realm of science."

"It becomes moral."

"Exactly! One of the ideas is that the cloned baby, once reaching maturity, may have the feeling that it lives a shadow life or that it was an experiment or that its life was already lived in the original in the brother or sister, whom it looks like. Such a person might lose interest in life or in his or her future. That sucks…I think it would be hard to discover that you have been manufactured from your brother's rib. Speaking of loss of autonomy…"

"Could this be solved by education?"

"Hmmm! A good lead…that's why I like these conversations with my darling Asian friend. Intuitively—as this is your playground—this child could reach the conclusion that he was given a gift and that consequently, he could be more responsible. Although—I get back to autonomy again—all that person's life, he would have the feeling that he would have something to pay, somebody to serve."

"Orrin, we Japanese live in a culture of service. This does not mean that we are cloned or servile; it is something we cultivate."

"It may be so, dear, but the story doesn't end here. Starting from the potential lack of appetite for normal life, the discrimination dispute rises from itself."

"Ooh, and who knows this ballad better…?"

"How subtle, my dear Yuzuki! You're *so* stuck up…there is the theoretical tendency of the parents to love their natural child more than the cloned one. It is the first level of discrimination; you just can't avoid it…well, it's hard to say."

Yuzuki suddenly became interested in the direction of their discussion.

"But human cloning is not a fact, is it?"

"No, but it's almost here."

"Meaning?"

"Scientists are making progress, but they encounter genetic anomalies. You get sick when you see the poor mice with teeth in their anus or with their internal organs grown on the outside. God has his rules, and I think we'll get a good slap here, no matter how much science evolves. It's something on a cellular level…I can't explain…something to do with genome segmentation, which you cannot perform over and over again without 'stirring' the genetic content. You play havoc with immunity."

"Fine, but if some parents want children and can't have them…genetic engineering could be a solution."

"I can see that you are really considering it."

"This is not about me."

Orrin could feel that his friend somehow voiced her thoughts, and he also knew that she did not refrain in front of him.

"Your subconscious is speaking now…you are aware of that, right?"

Yuzuki recognized that Orrin was somehow voicing her thoughts, knowing that she did not refrain in front of him. She tilted her head, accepting the diagnosis of "Doc" Hammett.

"If you want a baby, you can adopt one that was created the traditional way, damn it. Besides, darling, don't forget, I am always here for you. Look into my eyes: *I am here!*"

"Poor Orrin…I am sure they'll make some clones for your desperate hormones, too. Well, I don't know what you think, but I believe that as long as science helps reduce human suffering, why not? For me, this is just another stage in medical services."

"Let me doubt that, Yuzuki. What we are talking about here is replicating desirable characteristics. And the 'white' therapeutic part could also 'slip.' OK, we are not talking about chauvinistic tendencies but weight, height, and eye color. Not to mention the juicier parts: bust, midriff, bulgy biceps. These came to mean the 'better, choicer, more beautiful' people. That's not OK, I guess. Not to mention that you can produce more intelligent people. What about that, geniuses made to order? How would you feel, you who keep working even in your sleep, that somebody should pop up and have solutions for all the failures of science? Would you be happier to know that you no longer are as unique, as special, as you are today? And now I'm dead serious."

"Thanks for the compliment, Orry; if that was what you meant it to be…"

"You're welcome. We have a stratified society already. Polarizations galore…you want another one?"

Yuzuki had again lost herself in the maze of a field as fascinating as it was boring for her mind at the time.

"OK, OK…how do we stand from a religious point of view?"

"For the first time in history, the main branches—Christian, Mosaic, Hindu, Islamic, Buddhist—have reached a consensus: a definite *no.*"

"I see your mouth is dry. Would you like another drink?"

It was already too late. Yuzuki and Orrin had gone on talking while taking a walk. She had shown him Moscow, with everything in it; she took him to a ballet performance, and she took his picture with the Russian soldiers in Red Square, and then she sent him back to "sin land." At the airport, she felt she had to ask him when they would meet again.

But in the end, she just said, "Good-bye."

The Masters

She had had the chance of continuing to polish her Salmon in Moscow. Her mentor, Professor Moiro Takahashi, had guided her into her new direction.

"Yuzuki, I am an old school psychologist. I love the library, the sound and the smell of book pages. I liked the words of people in difficulty and my direct interaction with them; I was happy when I could bring back their smiles and their self-fulfillment. You work with different tools. I understand that the world seems to be taking you there. But I do not understand technology. Somehow…I don't want to understand it. I sense—and my intuition has never failed me—that your project has a brilliant future. Not under my guidance, though. But…"

Then he told her about Yuri.

His old Russian friend and colleague, Professor Yuri Kolotov, had started a program that was at least as daring as hers, at the State University of Moscow: interfaces and neuro-cybernetic processes.

"Yuri is working on a very ambitious project. What does he say? That there is a possibility of creating interfaces…don't ask me how…capable of communicating with the unconscious parts of our brains. Yuri claims that if people could get to know their blind spots, including the areas where he can be manipulated, then he would become less dependent on hazard and more reliant on self-consciousness. All the crises of humankind are based on herd instinct; therefore, rationalizing at an individual level might determine the formation of more reasonable expectations on a collective level. It is only a theory, of course, but I thought his work would complement yours."

The change had frightened her. Wasn't it enough that she had become isolated in her work? Now she had the "chance" of becoming totally estranged!

"Yuzuki, the only constant thing in life is change. Don't let doubt ruin your dream..."

The venerable Takahashi had to allow Yuzuki to "pick from the shelf," as they often joked. This was the role of a good psychologist: to help the subject choose the right way. Not the good way, but the best suited one.

"Do not forget, Yuzuki: everything is relative. And everything goes through a cycle. You catch the crest of the wave as you are moving..."

That had been the last thing he had told her face-to-face. Less than a year after she went to Moscow, Takahashi had passed away from a stroke. The irony of his life—abandoned by the body part he had taken care of all his life.

Tall, blond, and stocky, his blue eyes drilling into every detail, Yuri Kolotov had turned fifty and was glowing with professional achievements and daring projects. Gossip had it that he had been a KGB psychologist at the beginning of his career. Yet he had a nobility that contradicted the story of a hidden and sinister past; his voice was warm and his movements ample. But his eyes were keen and searching. The students often felt that Yuri could read their thoughts. The myth of his hazy past must have increased his authority as a telepath. His project was daring, maybe even more daring than Yuzuki's. He had exposed his theory to his friend Takahashi a while ago, and the old Japanese professor had reacted, as surprised as he was enthusiastic.

"Yuri, this is frightfully interesting! Do you realize that this tool could change the destiny of our profession?"

"It just takes it further, my friend. The world is heading toward a stage of self-control. I find it natural to give people the possibility to decide on their destinies before others do it for themselves only and possibly against the others."

"Actually, this interface of yours is a mind reader. How long will it take to fully develop it?"

"Long. I will need an apprentice, an 'apostle' to continue my work. I don't think I'll survive it."

"I won't either. But let me understand, Yuri; will it replace hypnosis?"

Professor Takahashi had a very comical way of asking questions. He spoke like a child and alternated words with many grimaces, onomatopoeia, and sudden swings of his body. He was aware of this "fault", but it was his trademark—the "base" on which he built trust in his interlocutors. There was a dose of enthusiasm and energy he put forth in his dialogues. Students used to call him "Yoda" or "Dalai Lama". And anyway, he was far too smart to feel injured by the reaction of the people who teased him for his "naughtiness."

"No, on the contrary, the mechanism I imagined looks for partial logical formations that are not expressed or are unconscious, beyond hypnosis. It should be able to read any spontaneous reasoning. Intuition. I believe that man's subconscious has predictive capacity, and we could use this to become... more rational."

"All right! And how are you going to materialize the contents of thoughts?"

"This is the hard part. I need an implicit "translator" which will transform the original information, as generated by electric impulses in the brain. And somehow, based on preset patterns closely correlated with our usual language, this information should be transposed into words, numbers, and diagrams, something easy to grasp or easy to process, with a margin of error, of course. Nothing is perfect."

"What would that mean, in practice?"

"An advanced system that can record cerebral data streams, with a few powerful servers—after all, we are talking about content storage—a database, and a self-teaching 'robot.' This is about artificial intelligence. It is a bit disturbing, Moiro."

"Lots of money, my friend..."

Yuri opened his eyes wide. It did not characterize him, but he was talking to a master "clown." And it was good fun empathizing with his friend.

"A few million dollars perhaps, a few good years. A dedicated team of three or four."

"Where can you get them?"

"The money, the years, or the people?"

Yuri had laughed nostalgically and lit his pipe.

"We shall see, old friend, we shall see. Would you like some more vodka?"

"Yes, please."

Takahashi never said no to one more glass. His brain had an enviable warning system; he knew when to stop.

Two years before, when he had met Yuzuki, Yuri had had reservations. Not about Yuzuki as a person or about her idea, but about the possibility that their projects might somehow intersect. The work base was fundamentally different, and the technologies and data processing instruments, too. The methods of interpretation were also widely different, and the applicability of results had completely distinct targets. After their initial discussion, Yuri changed his opinion, though. They had decided to talk via Skype. It was a good way of probing each other, and it agreed with their "wildness" mood and behavior.

"Where should I start?" he began.

"I ought to understand the goals of your project, both to figure out how I can help you and to see how I could join in with my research."

"All right, Miss Tanaka where do I want to get? To a reasonable dialogue with the human psyche, by deciphering the messages from beyond rational reasoning. And further on, to a sort of perpetuation of brain life. My vision is that in the future, we could have a sort of 'conclave' of intelligent minds, able to continue their creative existence beyond the collapse of the body."

"The first part, the dialogue with psyche, is clear. The second...I find it hard to imagine. I am a psychologist, basically, but functionally, I can hardly understand how a brain, be it that of a genius, could function after the physical death of the body that carries it. And particularly, why?"

"Imagine you have an old car whose engine is still functional, but whose gas pump is shattered, the body eaten with rust and the exhaust cracked…any comparison is allowed. But the engine still works. In theory, you can move the engine into a new car, where all the other components work. You could start at the first try."

"This if the chassis fits," Yuzuki cut in.

"Professor Takahashi warned me that you are a quick learner. The brain can function without a body. Medical cases have proven it. The coma is the best example. What is there to do? Attach artificial material support to a living brain. It need not be a standard human body. It must only simulate vital functions, maintaining the brain at its highest potential. Besides that, it should allow the brain to be active, not just for its vital functions but for the explicit manifestation of intelligence. The idea is that we should allow certain genius brains to 'exist' beyond their physical deaths. But in order to do that, we must first learn how to communicate with those brains autonomously."

"It makes sense up to a point, professor. But doesn't the mind need consciousness for the intelligent act itself? Can the brain be placed in a new box, with no personality? And then, how are you going to act? Will you disable that brain at some point, based on whose decision? At the end of the day, such an existence will depend on a switch."

"I have no answers to all these questions. There are nuances that elude me. I admit that one must equally work on the ethical aspect. This is a more sensitive matter. But going back to the first part of our discussion, an interface that can read thoughts can be built. Stephen Hawking is an example right now, both for the earlier metaphor of the engine and in connection to the equipment he uses to communicate— the synthesizer that helps him sustain a dialogue based on the movements of his head and of his eyeballs. That particular equipment uses a system of 'predictive' reading that only needs a few characters to finalize the word."

"I have always been fascinated by that system. Of course I am impressed with Hawking himself."

"Let's move on from this example, miss Tanaka. Think of comatose states or of temporary loss of consciousness or paralysis. In the end, we are psychologists, and we must have a therapeutic goal. At least, that's where I started, from the need to approach those clinical situations critical to the patients' lives, which we could solve by having a dialogue with an active brain whose supporting organism is reduced to a state where it is incapable of asking for help."

"Well, yes, in special medical cases, it makes a lot of sense."

"So without getting into detail, that's the idea: a decoder, a 'translator' of the electrical impulses of the brain, so as to understand what consciousness may tell us and the subconscious, too."

Yuzuki started making correlations. "So the stakes are: reading spontaneous manifestations predictively…?"

"Exactly!"

"Ah, that's what my project has at stake, too, Mr. Kolotov. Only on a collective level."

"Really, Miss Tanaka?"

"Please, call me Yuzuki."

Professor Takahashi had been right. Since Takahashi had understood the common root of both projects, Yuri felt that Yuzuki's presence was very useful for his project. She had explained her "story" to him: the duality of psychology/technology and the isolation of patterns. The basic principle was indeed the same, although the "raw materials"—individual intelligence and collective intelligence—were different.

"Perfect," said Yuri.

Yuzuki had in turn been happy to have found the person near whom she could finish her thesis, as Yuri understood her ideas and believed in them.

"At least we have the chance to compare the intermediate results and mutually support our theories, with good practice and arguments," he'd said.

"Even more, Professor, we can validate how well the unit replicates the characteristics of the whole."[3]

"Intuitively, yes, it makes sense."

Yuzuki had said her farewells to her father, the samurai sword maker who only worked by traditional techniques. They spoke on the phone once or twice a week. But she hadn't seen him in more than a year, since Professor Takahashi's funeral. Her mother's memory was alive anyway. Apart from that, she left nothing behind.

Going to Moscow seemed the natural thing to do.

---

[3] *Wikipedia*, s.v. "Fractal", http://en.wikipedia.org/wiki/Fractal

The Apprentice

As a postgraduate, Yuzuki had to have colloquies and seminars in an academic environment. Yuri had facilitated her access to a lecturer's position at the Department of Applied Psychology, within an experimental project on intuition training and development; it was optional in the university curricula, but it was perfectly suited to her goals.

Yuri had called the program "Mind Light". He had involved a few researchers and postgraduates interested in neural and psychoanalytic research: Russian, Chinese, Japanese—Professor Takahashi had been one. The program was developed through private psychology practices and through standard academic research. Once Yuzuki joined in, she had extended the research basis to the virtual area. The Salmon seemed to be the missing link in the chain that Yuri had imagined.

Yuzuki's experimental project implied educating the intuitive area of intelligence, which required a certain type of concentration, enhanced distributive thinking, and speed of reaction. Especially with first-year students, she often drew a parallel between the type of thinking of those who used information and the technique used in the handling of a *katana*.

"Incorrectly used, you can cut yourself with either 'weapon.'"

She had organized her courses as "mystery" games. Yuzuki's seminars were special. Her physique helped her; she was an exotic figure, young, delicate, and Japanese, with a natural gift of good speaking and high emotional intelligence. It came as no surprise, then, that in the almost two years since she had arrived in Moscow, she'd had a lot of "information swordsmen" attending her optional and apparently abstract course.

"So, what have you found interesting for me in the set of sources I mentioned?"

Andrey, one of her favorite students, raised his pencil firmly.

"Entropy!"

Yuzuki raised her eyebrows. "Ha, a true *katana* slice". And she cut the air with an imaginary sword. The feelings of isolation she experienced outside the university were fully compensated for by the ten or twelve hours of weekly lectures or debates. The students giggled.

"Can you develop your answer, Andrey? You know that in our seminar, neither whipping nor laurel crowning are accepted. Here you have the opportunity to say what you think, intuitively, even if it is not entirely correct."

Yuzuki wanted to discover Andrey's type of reasoning. He had found the right word for the theme in question. He was brilliant most of the time.

The exercise she was doing with the students aimed mainly at encouraging them to verbalize their first thoughts. Later, each student had the chance to logically analyze his or her first assertion or, on the contrary, to demolish it. Thus the students had to react quickly and predictively and above all, use their own brains.

"I have not found too much correlation in the sources. There's much confusion."

"'Much confusion," Yuzuki repeated.

"Yes. On Twitter, the new financial regulation framework is shattered, but no arguments are given. On facebook, things are heading toward comedy…the comments are simply without any content. Things change on LinkedIn; the debate is better focused but does not seem to have a finality. A conflict of ideas and nothing else."

Andrey riffled though his notes. He was the kind of student who, once "hooked", became a dedicated apprentice.

"In press sources…the criticism on Twitter persists here, too; analyses are contradictory, but they seem to be quite solid. You cannot reach a conclusion regarding the benefits of the new global financial system. Or at least, I couldn't. In the selected blogosphere, I can smell some more substance, only it looks biased in places."

"Biased. Andrey, please elaborate."

"It looks written to order. It is biased toward both sides. In the given sample, an advantage seems to appear on the side of those who advocate reform."

"What do you mean by advantage?"

"The weight of their arguments. I suppose that they prepared counterarguments in advance to the criticism that was going to appear. There is no hitch in their reasoning."

The "apprentice" settled more comfortably in his chair.

"The markets have been taken by surprise. Or rather, they haven't calibrated their expectancies very well. I believe…"

Andrey narrowed his eyes. His body language betrayed him; he was still fumbling, maybe because he had no logical argumentation; his typical way of reasoning.

"I think they haven't been consulted enough. This project was sort of presented to them."

"Why would you say that? You have just told me that it took them completely by surprise."

"Yes, well…there's also the resistance."

"Can you validate it? Or at least check it?"

Andrey looked again at the clusters of key words on the various sources. He scratched his head, rubbed his hands… Yuzuki felt the need to give him a helping hand. She sat on the chair near Andrey and started gazing at the screen too.

"What does your gut say?"

Andrey smiled, as if set free, and went on.

"I could isolate all the pros and cons of all sources, and at the end, I could compare them. Just to see if they all are in the same boat."

"Well, yes…" Yuzuki gave him another self-confidence trump.

"This way, we can see if their reactions are spontaneous or not."

"Super! You did delve into it. Did you also consult the content of the search engines?"

"No. Unfortunately…"

"As a rule, search engines are a good lead. Thanks, Andrey. Anyone want to add anything? Yes, Katerina?"

"There would be another angle: the presence of those against the new global financial program is more pregnant in certain media. They choose only verified media. Their comments are standard and implacable—no creativity there. Which is understandable…they are bankers or financial analysts."

The other students burst into laughter again. Katerina continued, "It's like a pack reunion. Speaking of what Andrey mentioned, resistance is complete. They don't even try to sketch a compromise. They seem blocked in their own world and their own wooden language. They are waiting for the previous normalcy to come back."

"Do the promoters of the reform seem more flexible?"

"Not necessarily…but they come with a new thesis, anyway, and against a generally negative background, they hardly need any flexibility at all. They simply bring forth an adjustment, and that suffices."

"Good. Were we able to reach a conclusion? Anyone may answer…"

Andrey volunteered; he felt bound to formulate the solution.

"I would say the new program will be adopted."

Katerina seconded him, and the others followed. Yuzuki smiled as if only to herself.

"As we discussed before, there is no perfect answer. We use random, unstructured, unstandardized information; the sources are in turn influenced from the start. Nonetheless… we could draw conclusions and plot tendencies based on them. All this in just one class! Yes, I also consider that the information analyzed leads to a favorable decision regarding the global financial program."

She allowed silence to set in, in the classroom and in the students' minds.

"Let's go back a little. The last time we met, I asked you a question. I also posted it on the course site, and I asked you to vote by a 'yes' or a 'no' during the class, on your laptops or tablets. Intuitively and ad hoc, ninety-two percent of you considered that *yes*, the new global financial program will be adopted. Do you remember?"

The students murmured affirmatively.

"Subsequently, after that question, your homework for today was to study a sample selected from the many sources I usually consult. You had twenty-three sources. I have about thirty-seven hundred. Based on the analysis of the content of the thirty-seven hundred sources, there is a possibility of eighty-nine point four percent that a new program will be adopted."

She stopped for a while, to allow them become aware of the effects of their exercise.

"And today, with Andrey's and Katerina's help, you have reached the same conclusion based on rational thinking. This means that, intuitively, you already had the answer, spontaneously and without any preliminary preparation. Or probably, you are in that credible mass that wants reform. In other words, you share the wisdom of the masses. Certain things are self-evident. By the way, this was an easy task. Only I was not interested in the solution Andrey found and that you validated. I am interested to see that you add to rational thinking, based on sources, what you get from inside. From your heart…"

She took another break to let their thoughts settle.

"This is what this course is about. Have an inspired day!"

The seminar ended in a humming of voices that kept the discussion going in smaller groups. Yuzuki went to Andrey.

"I liked that, Andrey."

"Thank you Yuzuki-San."

The eyes of the young Russian shone with enthusiasm and emotion.

"Have you decided on your final subject?"

"Not yet, I was thinking of postponing it for a year."

"But you are in your final year!"

All her life, Yuzuki had been racing against the clock. She had gotten her diploma in psychosociology at twenty-one, a year before the regular age. At twenty-three, she had received her diploma in cybernetic programming, after studying psychology in parallel for two years. At twenty-four, she had taken an intensive course in NLP[4] for almost a year. At twenty-six, she had her master's degree in artificial intelligence. At twenty-eight, she was back from Harvard after another master's degree in information technology and had started her PhD in Kanazawa, and then, shortly after, here at Lomonosov.

And Andrey, at twenty-two, twenty-three, was dreaming of a sabbatical year!

---

[4] *Wikipedia*, s.v. "NLP", http://en.wikipedia.org/wiki/Neuro-linguistic_programming

"That's true, but I do not want to rush. I would like to travel the world and see the various stages of development *in situ*. The Internet is fine, but it has its limits. It has no smell, no taste…"

"So you do have an idea connected to this subject."

"Not really, but I might get one on the way. Maybe you will help me with the final decision."

Oh, Generation Y!

Yuzuki had studied their patterns: independent people, eager for knowledge, critical, intellectually curious, egoless, anger-free, in permanent need of guidance, but not too loyal. She would have given one thousand years to see her own merits acknowledged, all the more since she had made it in a man's world. She hadn't missed any classes or any lectures, not during a single year! She had hardly missed an hour in her life; she had been dedicated to her vocation and to perfection.

And Andrey, an exceptional, intuitive mind, was ready to "skip" a valuable year, a year when things would probably change radically. New paradigms and new landmarks were sprouting; everything buzzed with effervescence. But this was irrelevant to Andrey.

"I don't see why I would hurry…"

His reaction came as a response to the silence of his teacher, who had concealed her shock quite well.

"I see…," she said.

Andrey continued, "I want to live concrete experiences, to meet real people. I want to do volunteer work in less developed areas. Interacting with this kind of experience is sometimes more useful than simply monitoring on the Internet how 'flocks' of people react based on the creed of other people, people they don't even know..."

Andrey did not realize that his last words could have a devastating effect on Yuzuki's feelings. She said good-bye to the brave young Russian. But she understood, after many years, why she woke up in the morning in an empty bed. Yes, she had neglected...no way, she had **ignored** the spontaneity of the people next to her. She suddenly realized that she simply did not have the capacity to sense the feelings of those people.

This only added to her anxiety.

II.

Excited by Bacchus and the music blaring in the boom box, she stripped naked and plunged into her large bed, which felt narrow and unfriendly for the first time. She felt smothered by the satin sheets; the pillows were too small or too soft, the wrinkles in her bed sheet prodded her body, and the night lights irritated her tired eyes.

She promised herself that she would never touch another drop of alcohol again. In the end, she managed to fall asleep. Her overactive body gradually slipped into immobility. She felt again that she was pulled off her bed by the angels' blast, rising out of her bed, her room, and the atmosphere, even higher, to the nothingness she had experienced before. This time, though, she felt she was floating among dim and remote lights. She slowed down, and just like the last time, silhouettes appeared in a light that had grown strong and aggressive.

They did not look like young and mischievous cherubs but like a gathering of the wise. The silhouettes looked like old samurai, bokken swords hanging at their waists, their hair in mage, *with long, white beards and moustaches, looking straight at her, with a hint of reproach, their eyes filled with wisdom and decision. There were seven of them.*

Why seven?

She needed to bow before them. She noticed that the cosmic wind had taken her naked, like she was when she had fallen asleep. She was ashamed in front of those fierce wise men of her dreams, and she felt like crying.

Then, in perfect sync, all the silhouettes put their hands out to her and kindly said, "Please stand, chosen soul. We are here for you."

She raised her eyes.

"Who are you?"

"We are the Listeners. We want to talk to you."

"I am far from anything familiar…what am I supposed to feel or say?"

"You should listen in your turn and try to understand."

She bowed again. This time she noticed that her body was wrapped in a silky white kimono.

Who has dressed me?

"I'm listening."

"We'll be back. We wanted to know whether you could see us. We know now that you can hear us, too—it's one more step forward."

"What shall I do?"

"Leave your mind open."

She felt frightened; it was the first time in her life she was talking to ghosts who apparently wanted to talk to her!

"Are you the ghosts of my forefathers, whom I did not honor properly?"

The seven wise men looked at each other and burst into laughter.

She felt that she was sliding quickly back to her familiar cosmos. This time, the fall was harsh.

She woke in the middle of the night, her head heavy, her body exhausted. She was naked again, the white kimono gone, feeling the cold of the night seep into her every fiber; she was thirsty, hungry, and cold.

Experiments

The phone was blinking hysterically on the nightstand. She had received a text message from Orrin: *"Got to talk. Urgent."*

Yuzuki texted back without hurrying: *"Get on Skype."*

She crawled to the other room, her "laboratory", and activated her public access key. In certain situations, she felt better if she used encrypted communication.

"What's happened, Orry?"

"I don't know if it's wise to speak on Skype…"

"We are on an encrypted path. Or have you developed a new way of transmitting, by telepathy?"

"Don't joke…this is serious."

"So, tell me the serious stuff."

Orrin put on a serious face. "It appears they've done the first human cloning."

"Last time you said it wasn't possible."

"But it is!"

"Where?"

"The Koreans. Southern, of course."

"Why of course? Why is it not in the media?"

"It's not official. When you enter this world, you don't always work in full sight. Anyway, apparently they worked undercover, under the umbrella of therapeutic research: the 'next level in medical research'. They had been working for a long time on regenerative cloning, but nobody thought of anything more than that; they did the reproductive cloning, too."

"Orry, I am tired, really, I don't understand a thing."

"You can find all this on the net; you are a specialist in advanced research…"

Yuzuki blew her top. "You've got a nerve…you call me in the middle of the night to inform me about I don't know what, and then you tell me to go and research. If you have a problem, you can explain it to me calmly and patiently. Otherwise, we'll talk tomorrow when I am awake and you ought to be sleeping."

"OK, OK."

Orrin took his tablet and sat down on the couch. Then he took a break, to make sure he had a good connection.

"Sorry I woke you up."

"I wasn't really sleeping. I've had these strange sensations lately."

"So…as I told you, cloning was developed for regenerative purposes, to obtain different types of tissue. The richest 'lode' for this field of research is that of stem cells.[5] One week after formation, the embryo is a cluster of about one hundred cells that, in theory, can become any type of cell. In practice, they used cloned embryos from which they harvested the stem cells."

"Doesn't that kill the embryos?"

---

[5] *Wikipedia*, s.v. "Stem Cell", http://en.wikipedia.org/wiki/Stem_cell

"It does! This is the problem. Back in 2007, they managed a replication with genetic material from monkeys—chimps. I wonder why?"

"They are the closest to humans…?"

"Exactly, Yuzuki: the structure of their genome is very similar to that of our genome. They presented it to the media as a cloning success. They didn't even call it that; they simply said it was 'genetic engineering' for reparatory and regenerative purposes. They listed a great number of conditions: heart attacks, plastic surgery, infertility, Down syndrome, leukemia, fibroses. The 'beauty' of this God game is that the stem cells thus harvested and cancer cells behave quite similarly. They can replicate blindly, and after the typical process of cell multiplication, they can accumulate similar mutations."

"I still don't understand why you are against the therapeutic option. Orrin. For a person who theoretically has no more chances…"

Yuzuki called forth her mother's last days. The pain, the despair, the fear for tomorrow…Orrin brought her back to the present:

"I didn't say I was against it. Only that for the time being, it is not stable. But I am totally against the idea that genetic engineering should lead to replicating people. Everything that was obtained through animal testing confirms that we cannot play with nature, Yuzuki. The pups were born bigger, with flawed vital organs. They grew old too fast, their immune systems were a mess…it's ironic, as one of the applications of therapeutic cloning could be to slow down the aging process. There are so many things that mankind should solve first and think of playing God later."

"Yes, maybe it's not a priority. But I can't help thinking of the couples who can't have children or of the young people with motor disabilities or other problems with their vital organs. Or, well, going further, maybe this way we could learn more. I think that in the end, if you get an improvement of, what do you call it, the 'totem' of our individuality…"

"But you don't need cloning for that. By the way, did you know that Japan has banned human cloning?"

"Well, yes…"

"Darling, you can't say that by cloning you take identity to the next level. I don't think we have to become upgradable in this way. I can see that: model Yuzuki two point two. Cloning cannot recreate memories, dreams, prestige, fear, curiosity, empathy, emotion…a person is identified not only by his or her genetic material, but also by a unique consciousness. Hell, you are a psychologist…"

"If we don't understand certain things, it doesn't mean they are not achievable or possible. You are a scientist too. How many times has nature rendered you speechless?"

Yuzuki felt she was losing control. She was tired, and Orrin was adding troubles to her mood.

"You can't say that everyone involved means ill, Orry. I am persuaded that nothing in this world can be fully controlled. Look at nuclear energy."

"My dear, in your wish to antagonize me, you touched the exact critical spot. Once this technique is under control, an unprecedented supremacy can appear, and the access won't be like it is in your projections, widely open. You won't see therapeutic cloning used for tens…hundreds of thousands of lives in the poor communities of the globe. Get the message! Through genetics and cloning, people won't get any better, right?"

"OK, OK, don't get all flustered. You are right about that. It is really possible that powerful nations will take advantage of that. Sociologically speaking, it looks like a real threat."

"Thanks, you finally put your clever—and beautiful—head to work."

Yuzuki smiled, embarrassed. She didn't know how to accept a compliment. So she replied awkwardly, "Are you more relaxed now?"

"Somewhat. Anyway, thanks for listening, Yuki."

"You haven't called me this for a long time."

They both kept quiet for several seconds. Yuzuki started again, more quietly:

"Since we are here…how do they do it, technically?"

"What?"

"Cloning…"

"I don't know the details. In science, it is called 'nuclear transfer of somatic cells.'"[6]

"It sounds…let's drop it."

"Let's put it differently. Assuming you want to have a baby with your genetic characteristics and assuming you can't have babies…"

"*No…and no!*"

---

[6] *Wikipedia*, s.v. "SCNT", http://en.wikipedia.org/wiki/Somatic-cell_nuclear_transfer

Yuzuki seemed terrified at the thought. But Orrin went on: "Assuming! We take a sample, a cell...it contains your genetic material. We take out the nucleus. Then we take a fertile stem cell, from a couple, and take that nucleus out and insert yours instead. Then we put the new cell to work: some ultra-violet light, more proteins to stimulate division, and *abracadabra*...that's it. We take the new cell and put it back in your womb."

"Then...you can do that?"

"You may be sterile, but that doesn't mean your womb cannot carry a pregnancy. Of course, you can use a surrogate mother. In theory, after nine months, a baby is born from a cell with a 'Yuzuki' nucleus. That's all there is to it."

Yuzuki was stunned. "Why would a mother accept that?"

"Well, *voila...*"

Yuzuki was thinking and talking beyond Orrin's words. "So by cloning, either therapeutic or reproductive, you change the destiny of the human embryo very early. You don't kill it, but you change its destiny...its core. You take from it the chance of being what it was supposed to become."

"Good girl, you've got it. If only everybody thought like you."

"And...this has been done already?" Yuzuki asked with a shiver.

"Yes, it has."

"You mean, they manipulated the cell, and...it worked?"

"Even more than that: the first cloned baby was born."

Feelings...?

She made a lemonade before going to bed. She looked through a few magazines—fashion magazines. It wasn't really a concern, but...then she listened to some Russian recordings for a few minutes. She had made progress but still needed daily repetitions if she wanted to catch up with the Russian students and professors, to be able to think like them. Before getting nestled in her bed, she read part of her messages.

She stopped at Orrin's: *"Don't you miss me?"*

She smiled and shivered.

"I can't afford it..."

Later on, she fell asleep. Deep sleep. Deeper than ever. She didn't even turn the lights off. She dreamed a lot. More than ever. Lots of light. She woke up. Again bathed in light. Spring sunlight. The most brilliant sun of that spring.

8:37 a.m.?

It was almost nine o'clock. She had a lecture at nine. It was the first time in a long while that she had woken up so late, although she had had that dream for only a few minutes. It had happened so fast…and was so good. She sat on the edge of the bed, numb, eyes raised to the sun. A few tears trickled down. Not from tiredness. Not because of the sun. She was crying with happiness. Finally…

She reset herself.

What will my students say? I have never been late…

She walked into the classroom after 9:15 a.m. She gently put her bag on the desk. She was still in a state of relaxation and partial indifference, a mood she had experienced in her childhood. The students didn't seem too affected by the fact she was late. Or didn't let that be seen. And she managed to finalize the class in time, even though she had started late. She felt her voice run differently. The students also felt her apparent lack of strength. Some thought it was a test. Yuzuki was a master of surprises.

She walked to her desk and, giving a deep sigh, rubbed her face and eyes with her little white hands, her eyes still clear from last night's dream.

"Everything OK, Yuzuki-San?"

She was frightened. Andrey…

"Yes, yes, I had a…long dream, longer than usual. I hope my coming late…"

"It happens all the time."

"Really? I thought professors were always on time."

"Not all of them." Andrey tried to catch her eyes, while she kept them glued to the floor. "Yuzuki-San, I wanted to talk to you about something. Do you have a minute?"

She looked at her tablet, confused. Where was her planner? She was still numb from the dream. What a beautiful dream!

"I have a pretty busy day today. But tomorrow morning I'll be in my office…"

"Well…I wanted to suggest a more relaxed talk…about my journey. I have started to organize my itinerary, and I wanted to ask you a few questions about Japan: what would be worth seeing, reading, knowing beforehand…some guidance."

A more relaxed talk…Yuzuki did not have such a notion. With her, dialogues were intense, professional, and academic. Only with the late Takahashi had she allowed herself to be less intense, but their conversations had still been about her profession or about the limit between science and trivia. Today, though, she couldn't think. She didn't feel like thinking. She had to follow her heart… wasn't this what she kept telling her students? It was time to try something more flexible, especially in the relationships with her students. Although Andrey was not just a student.

Why not? A relaxed talk…

"Today at thirteen hundred? How does that sound? We'll have lunch in the university park. Do you like sushi?"

"Yeah, sure, at thirteen hundred. Sushi, all right…"

She had found a restaurant where they made that Japanese delicacy as it was made back home, and they delivered to one's home as well. Or in the park. The sushi was expensive, like everything else in Moscow, but it kept much of the freshness of Japanese sushi.

The wild apple trees in the university park were in full bloom. They reminded her of the school days when she was still wearing a uniform. Spring…her explosion of life, year after year. And that celestial dream had filled her heart with a feeling of complete yielding, a total abdication from rules and programs.

Her talk with Andrey fulfilled an exceptional day. She decided not to work at all that day. She forgot about her planner, her project, and why she was at Lomonosov. She wandered the streets of Moscow, reliving those frissons with each step she took, fresh like the tree buds and sheer like the spring wind.

She checked her messages as usual before bed. Orrin had not answered her message. Yuzuki wished herself to sleep, hoping to go on another angelic trip. But she woke the next day after a regular night with no revelations and no stopovers in magical realms. Neither the next night, nor the fourth, nor the fifth…she was back to normal with her sleep. That was good news. But her enthusiasm turned to anguish; she experienced a feeling of paradise lost.

Orrin's answer finally arrived. After one week?

"My dear, sorry for the delayed message. I met a girl. And since then, I haven't checked my mail regularly; I just read the urgent messages. I don't want you to feel I abandoned my friends, but believe me, I've lost my head…
Got to go now…we'll talk.

P.S. Big scandal with the Korean clone…apparently it only lived for three months…so?"

So…what? What did dear Orrin want to tell her? He could only answer urgent messages…she was categorized as "we'll see after a week of sex…?"

How the hell can a relationship like this that flares in the first week, resist? And then what was the big deal about giving me a quick and simple answer? He could have called me; was he really stuck to the…machine? What is this woman made of? And why is he telling me this? Since when am I the confidant of his liberated love? Another sleepless night…

She poured herself a glass of wine and then another. Her frustration drained away with the red liquid until the mingy bottle claimed the wine was gone. She had emptied it in less than fifteen minutes. This was probably faster than the body was used to absorbing and the brain to accepting.

She woke up naked, her skin in goose bumps over the shivering flesh. She felt the alcohol seeping behind each pore. She put on whatever she could find handy and ran to the kitchen. She put the kettle on for some tea and ate some chocolate she found in a cupboard. The fridge was almost empty. She found some stray fruit. Enough.

She dropped the jasmine teabag into the steamy cup and took the rest of the chocolate and hid again in her large bed. She left the lights on in the hallway. This time, her meeting with the dream had been harsh; she swore again that she was no longer going to drink more than half a glass. She'd had enough of this madness. She grew calmer and began to rationalize, aloud, looking up to the ceiling, as if she wanted the "listeners" to hear.

"It was only a dream—today and a week ago. I am neurotic…I work too hard; I am alone. I miss Orrin, and he's having an affair right now. What does he care how I feel? Damn, what's with these thoughts?"

She was warm now, so she left the bed. It was not 5:00 a.m. yet. She activated her Salmon and assigned them a new task: "human cloning." She activated all engines and networks and determined the selection criteria for the academic and nonacademic blogs and forums.

ENTER!

The Salmon were flying from one knot to another in the mission entrusted by their creator, to look for the right connections. They had already started to isolate key terms: embryo, ethics, fertility, DNA, spindle cells, freedom, risk, death…

As the Salmon dug into the virtual cosmos, the screen gradually filled with graphs and text syntheses on the structure decided by Yuzuki. Ideas about cloning had turned up everywhere in the world, from the USA to New Zealand, from South Africa to Norway, from Germany to South Korea, and even farther, to Japan.

What was Orrin about when he said Japan isn't into genetics?

Russia seemed to be the only one to have openly opposed this type of research over time, and the country had even forbidden all types of experiments by presidential decree. Did Orrin know this? Maybe if he did, he wouldn't be so passionate and would understand that there was space for affinities even with the big "numb enemy of the East."

The Salmon had finished searching. The list was long. But their work was just beginning…it was a good bridge; she could help Orrin with some preliminary conclusions.

Orrin! Orrin!

He kept popping into her mind, obsessively, and that intrigued her. She could control herself, couldn't she?

Yuzuki put an end to her daydreaming. And yet, her meetings with the angels were too well delineated to be only a sick figment of her imagination. They looked like more than a banal manifestation of her subconscious.

She walked to the big bedroom window. The clouds had gathered above the university tower, in the giddy morning light. It was probably going to rain steadily for a few days. That was Moscow at this time of year. She took her *tatami* out of the cabinet, and for a whole hour, she did her Reiki exercises. She needed them badly.

A few days passed, and then she got a message from Orrin.

"My dear, you blew my mind. It's like you were truly drunk…spelling mistakes aside, what did I do wrong? I have always admitted I am pretty hormonal. But I don't feel

gross or hypocritical, as you gave me to understand that was how I treated you. I am surprised that my message offended you so badly.

"*Still, you were right: we broke up two days ago after two weeks of crazy sex. Obviously, not because the 'bimbo' was a two-bit tramp, but because, surprisingly (or not) she preferred her ex-boyfriend, and she went back to him. Otherwise, she was a really great girl.*

"*Now...I need to get something clear. Paradoxically, to be honest, your message both surprised and pleased me. Somehow I felt for the first time that you cared about me and my feelings for you.*

"*Maybe, given this unexpected moment of sincerity, it wouldn't be a bad idea that on our next meeting, we should be more open with each other. More American style, how about this?*

"*Yuki, let's stop teasing...I would like to know whether your morale is high and your state of mind is carnival-like...as I knew you: merry, lively, stimulating. O.*"

Then she sat down at her desk, and for the first time, she didn't look at the reports of her Salmon; she opened her mail. She had to write a message that was, what...thirty years too late?

She needed to know that someone had a minimum amount of affection for her. She would have liked it to be love, perhaps, even if she was not very sure of her feelings; she wasn't good at pursuing them either. She had no idea how to show them, in fact. She read the message again where she had scolded Orrin and felt embarrassed.

Feelings...?

When the hell did I write this trash?

Yep, it was clear that it had been after that bottle of wine. Yes, the message was full of mistakes. And yes, it was clear that behind the poisoned words, there lurked the passion of many repressed emotions, sentimental and sexual frustrations—the passion of her solitude, on which she had grown ever more dependent.

Am I in love with Orrin? Or is he only my comfort zone...?
How many other men have I met, to know how it is?

She thought too much. She knew too much about how her brain worked and how those electrochemical sparkles behind the thoughts acted.

Sometimes too much knowledge is damaging...

She took a long time before sending the message.

"Dear Orrin, I badly miss our talks! Y."

It didn't sound good. What was that, a memo? Was that what she wanted Orrin to discover? She changed it and released it into the Internet clouds before she changed her mind...

"I miss you! Y."

She giggled like a schoolgirl. Then she dressed carefully, put on some *Annayake* perfume, and floated slowly to the university.

She was to meet Yuri.

III.

She snuggled in her bed. It didn't seem so large and empty any more. She clutched her pillow and moaned gently to herself and to her muddled dreams. As if on purpose, silence descended on her, and she fell into the deep sleep she had become accustomed to over the past few weeks.

She felt again enveloped by a smooth light, like liquid velvet, which caressed her tired body and relaxed her tight nerves. Then the heat turned into a soft, warm breeze that opened up her fetal body.

She felt that she was flying face-up. Light surrounded her, and she felt how her body stood on an imaginary ground. Although she was aware that she was asleep, she woke, in her dream or whatever state that was, in a cherry orchard in full bloom. The pinkish-white petals were everywhere—in trees and under them, floating in the air.

She took small, tentative steps toward the middle of the orchard. She expected the visions of her former dream to turn up from behind the trees. Only nothing happened. Neither cherubs nor samurai disturbed her walk in the orchard...

A few minutes later, if this was how time was measured there, she noticed a simple stone bench and a woman sitting on it. She drew closer, and as she came near, her breath became more elaborate. Every fiber in her body was tight with emotion…

The woman was dressed in a white kimono; she was young and reminded her of…

No, this can't be true…

"Mother?"

"My girl, you've grown. You are a woman now…"

"Mother? Is that really you?"

"This is what you want to see, so yes, it's me. Please sit down."

She felt tears bathing her hot cheeks and her body emptying of the suffering at the loss of her mother. She had lost her when she was only twelve. Nobody had known how to explain to her and to her father why it had happened. Why so sudden? Why so young?

"My dear, we don't have much time. I would like you to listen to me."

"Yes, Mother."

"You are chosen, and you must be honored that you have been chosen. You will come here more often in the near future."

"Am I ill?"

Her mother's ghost shook her head.

"I knew it. Am I going to die?"

"No, far from that. You are safer than ever. Take it as an initiation. Those at the edge of the orchard need a chosen person—like you."

"Yes, Mother. How can I help them?"

"You know better…that's what they say, that you know what you have to do."

"But…"

"There isn't time for much talk. I want to look at you a little longer. You are a gorgeous woman."

Their teary eyes were focused on each other.

"You will have your own children. Enjoy them as much as I enjoyed you."

"Mother, but you didn't tell me…"

"I love you, baby, I love you very much!"

"Mother…"

Her mother's image turned into cherry petals that were blown away by a gentle breeze. Unlike on her former journeys, this time the return was smoother. She stayed in the orchard awhile longer, enjoying the harmony of its colors. This could only be heaven, and her mother was there. It couldn't be any different.

She woke up fresher than ever—partly regretting, partly reassured. She knew it was the last time she was going to see her mother so vividly and so close.

The Portal

Yuri was working hard on his "toy." He hadn't reached any palpable result, because he had not dared look for a volunteer. He would have offered himself…but he needed someone at the "play station" so as not to turn the experiment into a grotesque scientific event. He needed somebody who would understand all those sophisticated rituals that activated the latent areas of the brain, but somebody who was also able to stop them in time. He was under a lot of stress. Time flew by. And this really pissed him off.

He hadn't talked to Yuzuki for a week; he hadn't found time, and she didn't seem to be herself. As coordinator of Yuzuki's thesis, he had to prepare a set of preliminary conclusions for her second colloquium. But his thoughts were stuck with what *she* was supposed to do for his project.

Selfish…as usual.

Yuzuki tiptoed into his lab. Unlike her sanctuary, Yuri's laboratory was a jungle. She looked with amusement at the papers lying everywhere, on desks, on walls, under desks, on chairs, and among the books in the small bookcase. Pictures and images of colored brains, diagrams and mental charts, formulae, and programming schemes rounded up Yuri's organized chaos.

A few scattered pipes, proclaiming he was using them all, according to…maybe no rule. And a couple of half-hidden bottles of vodka. To pep up.

Yuzuki helped him assemble the system that lay at the basis of the entire portal: servers, data bases, and communication protocol. Yuri had focused on the probe designed to read whatever the subconscious of the volunteer subject would say.

The probe was practically a membrane, like a swimming cap, with a multitude of small electronic devices sprouting variously colored wires connected to a number of monitors. Yuri also needed scenarios for the "assault" and for coming to after hypnosis, but mainly for the time in between those two, when the subject was going to be "stationed" in a sort of controlled coma. The "assault" was the two-step hypnosis. The first stage was a standard hypnosis. The second, Yuri's innovation, was to establish "contact" with the subconscious, which involved the "scaling" of the rational area of consciousness. He was going to build these scenarios for all subjects, based on their life experiences, pleasant and unpleasant memories, loved ones, worries, fears, and other things known only to the subjects. On the basis of this, by means of the "assault," Yuri was going to reach his destination—so far unknown.

"Yuzuki, it's so good to see you! You look very fresh today…"

"I've had a confusing time recently, if that's what you mean. I'm fine now. How are we?"

"Pretty good. There's still some work to be done on the scenarios...the probe is ready in theory...I should rent the servers...and of course, there's the subject. I haven't made any progress in that respect. I couldn't identify a suitable case at the clinic. I don't think anyone is suitable, as I had first thought. I think we need a strong, healthy brain."

Yuzuki smirked, "Consider the problem solved."

"Do you have somebody in mind?"

"Yeah, I'll be your interface."

"Yuzuki, you know how risky it is. This has never been done before..."

"And who do you think you'll find willing to jump without the spare parachute? There's got to be a 'first time.'"

"Not you, though..."

"Yuri, we are scientists. This is our arena and our altar. What do I have to lose?"

"It is very risky..."

"It's what I want. If you wish, I can sign a paper."

"Are you sure, Yuzuki?"

"Very!"

Yuri pondered for a while. Yuzuki was the ideal solution. How could he not have thought of this already, even theoretically?

"Yes, I will need your formal consent...although, paradoxically, we won't be able to work officially...at least not in the beginning."

"I don't think it's necessary. So what else can I do to move on?"

"Well, help me with all the installation, revise my scenarios and…finally, tell me all the nice or most hidden things about yourself. All of that could help me bring you back if, God forbid, something happens. Anything…we must work on your brain for the implant as well."

"Come again?"

"I must show your brain a vast repertoire of terms. The probe will capture an impulse from your brain for each of these terms. I practically built the portal database with pairs of word-thought, so it will be able to perform the translation. It needs, so to say, your pattern of thinking and conceptual association."

"And how are you going to get that?"

"I'll need you for a few good hours for the next few days. I'll practically fix a visor above your eyes and the probe on your head, and I will show you on the visor display thousands of words, terms, *syntagmas*…maybe hundreds of thousands. As it 'sees' them, your brain will process them and will generate specific impulses; the probe will capture these and will transmit them to the translator in pairs, as I said before. This way, it will learn how you associate those terms. I hope it will."

"Will you implant the definitions, too?"

"No, only flashes of words and terms. Your brain should process them instantaneously, independent of your reasoning and understanding. We'll have a dead zone as well… terms you don't know or don't understand or for which your mind makes no connection. It is just an extended application of the photo-reading technique, OK? It will be pretty hard, because, as you may well imagine, I made the first version of the translator in Russian; that's why it is highly likely you won't perceive everything. I don't speak Japanese...so we'll need to have a conversion. I thought of going with English, as it's somewhere in between. And anyway, it's the language we two use to talk..."

Yuzuki remembered Orrin's words: *"Everybody speaks our language."* He was right, the condescending...

Even here, she wasn't free of him.

"That makes sense. I understand Yuri: you are going to search my brain thoroughly."

"Something like that..."

They talked until late at night. They only stopped for a brief lunch at the university cafeteria, which didn't have much on its menu. But they appeased their hunger.

Yuri was writing diligently. He had already filled a notebook with his ideas. As he listened to her, he was amazed at the course of her life. He realized how valuable Yuzuki the subject was, beyond Yuzuki the person.

The following week, they started on the technical side. Yuzuki created a backup system, to provide continuity in case the main application got stuck or came up with errors. They rented processing volume in the cloud,[7] offered by a Japanese giant in the field of technological services, and she tested the system again, step-by-step, detecting the source's subconscious and making real contact with it and also detecting the exchange of messages, message translation, synchronization, and recording, as well as a load of other technical details.

---

[7] Refer to cloud computing; *Wikipedia*, s.v. "Cloud Computing", http://en.wikipedia.org/wiki/Cloud_computing

For another few days, they trained for the use of the probe. Initially, Yuri checked to see how open Yuzuki was to hypnosis. After a few awkward attempts, they managed to penetrate the first "line of defense." This was what they called the mental blockages and protections of those who, being aware of the process, resisted unconsciously.

Later, he had Yuzuki check her health. Aside from some minor digestive issues, everything was all right.

Then came the probe checkup: reading the primary cerebral signals, the brainwaves of the young Japanese's mysterious mind. Yuzuki's brain responded well, unhesitatingly, with sharp, accurate answers.

All they had left to do was the first "assault."

At last!

Yuri took the probe and carefully placed it on Yuzuki's head. Wide-eyed, she gave him a nervous smile. Yuri blinked hearteningly. His kind eyes soothed hers, as much as they could in such adrenalin-laden moments.

The hypnosis went smoothly, without a hitch. Then Yuri started the music, as decided. Yuzuki had preferred Bach's Air.[8] Every three minutes, a sequence of key words was inserted, following her life story.

A few minutes had passed before Yuri could capture the first curve on the monitor. He was overwhelmed. It was his first live immersion on a subject—his colleague. The flow was constant and consistent. He recorded the signals on several discs. He didn't know how good the translation program was yet, but anyway, he was receiving a communication flow that he could study, and this was the best news for the moment.

Ten minutes had passed since the first impulses. He had managed to isolate a few patterns when the machine monitoring the state of his "patient" went astray. Yuzuki's pulse shot much above the acceptable limits. Yuri looked at the table where his young colleague lay; the numb body seemed to be

---

[8] "Air–Johann Sebastian Bach" (video posted by 2010NEBELWARNER, January 25, 2010) *YouTube.com*, http://www.youtube.com/watch?v=rrVDATvUitA

vibrating with a gentle motion, which gradually turned into a rigid shiver. Her eyes showed white under the half-closed eyelids, and her breathing was erratic.

Yuri abandoned the console of the system and started running the waking scripts.

"You are in a cherry orchard in bloom.
A gentle spring wind blows among the flowering trees.
Your father is in a corner of the orchard, with a group of samurai.
Behind them, a young woman sitting on a bench is smiling. She is your mother.
White-skinned angels fly in circles above the orchard and play Bach on their harps."

Yuri looked at the console to which Yuzuki was connected. Her pulse was dwindling. At a certain point, in fact, it became so weak that Yuzuki risked going into cardiac arrest. Yuri's panic went beyond everything he had experienced before. He repeated the scenario more eloquently, alternating it with an unspoken prayer. But the heart of the young Japanese girl seemed indifferent.

He left aside all procedures, scenarios, and prayers and came closer to the table where Yuzuki was lying and to the table where the defibrillator and the adrenalin syringe had been set aside before the experiment. He tried a classic resuscitation.

"Come on, Yuzuki, come on! Leave the seraphim and the orchard and come home!"

Time was running against her. Yuri was red with effort and with anguish. He only had three minutes, and two were already gone. After a few failed maneuvers, he lost it; he took the adrenalin syringe and very precisely—his only valid reflex—stabbed the slowing heart.

Yuzuki started wildly, with an ample, noisy breath. She opened her eyes wide, with a moist, hysterical look. For a while, she breathed heavily, with loud, panic-laden moans. Yuri took her head between his hands and started pressing her temples and her eyes carefully, massaging them in his own personal way, until gradually Yuzuki came back to normal. The pulse had stabilized. She was breathing normally and had gotten a minimum of vitality back. But she looked exhausted and could barely articulate. In between sighs, she managed to talk to Yuri.

"I wanted to stay…"

"For God's sake, how did you think of that?"

"Only when you are there can you understand…otherwise you can't…it's so clean…so sublime…yes, I wished… I wanted to stay there."

"Why, Yuzuki?"

"I don't know…I only know I didn't want to leave."

"Did you hear or feel my presence?"

"I heard you, Yuri. I felt you…you were smiling and waving at me to come to you."

"That was no smile, Yuzuki. And why didn't you come back?"

"I had gone too far; I saw you too late. I had no reason to come back."

"What do you mean, you had no reason?"

Yuzuki tried to sit up. Yuri helped her sit at the edge of the bed. She noticed her blouse undone, her torn bra, and the small puncture where a little drop of blood had trickled. She looked at Yuri with wondering eyes, and he confirmed her suspicion.

"I had to activate you somehow…"

They both smiled, embarrassed. Yuri was more bitter and still agitated inside. Yuzuki took a sip of water and then walked to the door.

"We'll talk tomorrow. I need to rest now."

"I cannot let you leave like this… You've just been in a cardiac arrest. You should see a doctor."

"You are a doctor, Yuri."

"Yes, but not a heart one… I've just made some basic examination. Really, we have to make sure that there is no lasting harm done. I am not sure yet if I want to continue with this" and Yuri pointed the computer and the "resurrection" table.

"Trust me! All I need is a long, healthy sleep. I will go to the doctor tomorrow.

"Promise me, Yuzuki!"

"I do…"

"All right, we'll talk tomorrow."

Yuri took one of the bottles of vodka and took a long sip and then another one; his body was still shivering. On the one hand, he shivered because he had been close to losing Yuzuki, but on the other because he had succeeded in reaching the waves of her subconscious.

At last!

Crazy day…

After a half hour of scattered thoughts, he washed his face, poured some water on his head, and took a cup of coffee from the machine near the lab's kitchenette. He turned back and got the system out of hibernation. A second important stage came next—brainwave translation. In several folders, he had saved a few hundred gigabytes of impulses transmitted by Yuzuki's mind. He transferred these onto the decoder's server and launched the translation procedure.

The system was running slowly; he clearly needed more resources. He let it run at its own pace, afraid that he might overcharge it and waste the meager results obtained so far. He lay down on the narrow couch in his office and promptly fell asleep.

So did Yuzuki, as soon as she got home. They both slept like babies until noon the next day. They had restocked on courage and confidence.

They sensed that an awesome adventure was coming.

Fine Tuning

Yuri woke suddenly with the fresh memory of the last day's experiment. He was a little woozy. He landed straight on the decoder chair. A few screens were full of words, unrelated in places, but coherent for the most part. He skimmed several sequences and started all over again. Then he exported them in a format that was easier to edit. The process took a few seconds, and then he printed the few pages.

He had gotten to the second page when he realized that he was reading a dialogue; it was obvious from the turn of the phrases.

He read again, more carefully.

"* ¤t ank you for accepting to communicate with us. We chose this nco nter to come b ck to you through a mess ger you know, you tr sted xnd thanks to 444 4e und stood that you are the ri::: person Master>

xactly #hope you have progressed with your work.i trust you...manage to ca;;;y it out suc?es*fully especially since you have beside you a character as curious and intelligent as y>urs //my new partners need an interlocutorThey want to sent theirmessages and would like ¤¤¤¤¤

learneddddd// or at least for reflection#

◻◻ ◻◻◻◻◻◻◻◻◻◻◻◻◻◻◻◻◻◻◻◻◻◻◻◻◻◻◻◻◻◻◻◻

#I will wait for you to tell me if you agree with this dialogue, particularly since we don't know whether >>>remember our discussion once you are back in your universe, awake# we wouldn't like to waste your energy. It must become a cycle of conversations# _ we don't know whether this modality is # suitable, maybe on our next meeting in this spa2e you will tell us ::: we have this possibility >

A way to receive the thoughts or sensations I might > have during sleep, this as far as our◻ tool is efficient>>>>>>>>>> >>>>>>>>>>>>>>>>>>>>>>>>>>>>>>>>>>>>>> >>>>maybe it would be better if you told me what you want to communicate and I will te___ meeting #if I understand or if we have an answer for you but..."

Then came a sequence that the translator hadn't been able to render or simply hadn't understood. It was clear that they had to do some more work on the interpretation protocol. It was also clear that the problems had to do with the language used. Hence, there were many bizarre associations, maybe even illogical, either in Yuzuki's mind or decrypted by the translator.

Anyway, it seemed that at least from a logical point of view, the translation was accurate, and this was a winner. Communication with Yuzuki's mind was coherent, undistorted by irrational thoughts that any mind "generates" by hazard or due to an erroneous perception of reality.

He went on reading from where the translator had managed to render a fluent dialogue.

"m aster please take me with you[> MPOSSIBLE my dear,,,we cannot keep you in this space so long because it is not suitable to your]#☐te............

But ple"e, this is my chance!>

It is not time for you to leap must be postponed<<<<<

But may!be now is the time to come home. i miss home i want to stay , "33#3#33#333#-3# >>>> but this is your mind, you can find more easily, this is not the way nor themoment you must wait for your moment it's not here yet and we don't think it is for the beXter to part with your own.

Your mission is very important for your soul and for us.

*::::::::::::::::*_____

_____ *"*

The communication stopped abruptly. It was probably the moment when he had started to resuscitate Yuzuki. Yuri pondered for a few minutes. Then he rose and went to the corridor. He needed a breath of fresh air. He went back to the lab, took the papers with him, and sat on the nearest and best shadowed bench near his lab building.

He remained there for many minutes, fraught with emotion. Adrenalin was still bubbling in his veins. His years of work were bearing the first fruit, but the episode with Yuzuki on the table, so close to death…this he couldn't stomach.

Spring was almost gone; the blossoms had scattered. Around him, nature was changing, as was his state of mind.

He quickly did his regular "cleansing," knowing how dangerous it was to let his thoughts and morale slide toward lack of confidence. Yuri had his "gray" spots too; hence this ritual.

Yuzuki walked down the alley, like a redemption. Her eyes were puffy with sleep or maybe with the previous day's experience, but she looked calm.

"Are you all right, Yuri?"

Yuri looked at her with beseeching eyes. His kind face showed confusion and restlessness at the same time. He gave her the papers. Yuzuki read in one gulp. At the end, she, too, was confused, but she seemed urged and motivated by what she had read.

"I know where the weak spot is. I know what we did wrong. The scenario is completely unsuitable."

"What do you mean—wrong? It is based on what you told me you had lived…your visions…those cherry tree illusions, the cherubs…I had to create a state of comfort for you, starting from those visions, that made you feel well, that boosted your confidence…"

"That's exactly it. My comfort was increased by your intervention. Probably your attempt at getting me out of hypnosis only pushed me even further toward that state…"

"But you drafted it…"

"Don't feel guilty, Yuri; we are in this together…"

"…but you could have died! Or become a vegetable forever. How do you think I would feel?"

Yuri burst into tears. The kind Russian, the star of Lomonosov in neural networks, seemed crushed under the impact of failure. Yuzuki put her hand around his shoulders.

"Yuri, what is the basic law of science?"

"Law…what law?"

"Trial and error!"

"You could have died on my table, in my lab, under my eyes! This would have been an error…"

"Are you afraid of this?"

"Yes!"

"Then it's probably time for us to stop. I cannot take the next step without the help of this tool's creator. You are just one step away from talking to my other side, the unseen, unknown side, that nobody understands, not even myself—consciously—and you are afraid…What of? What people would say? Where is that damned paper with my consent?"

"In my office."

"Next time, pin it up above the computer and focus on what is important."

Yuzuki shrugged his shoulders.

"On the *solution*, Yuri! On the solution. We now have enough data to fine-tune the system and the scenario…"

"I think we need more processing power…"

"We'll buy it; we'll make it ten times, a hundred times bigger…you said you were still within the budget…"

"Yes."

"What else do we need?"

"I don't know. I have just printed these papers. I slept until an hour ago."

"Me too, and I'm stronger than ever. Now I know how the return scenario must be."

"Are you sure?"

"Yes. The script must get me back *here*, Yuri!"

"Yes, that's fine…"

"We need anchors and landmarks in my real life, things that make me happy and content here. I don't know how many there are, but at least we have a starting point. My work, my garden back home…the person I think I love… coffee…I don't know! We have a place to begin."

Yuri was surprised. "You have a boyfriend?"

"I don't know yet…but that's not important now."

The professor looked at her with more confidence. He needed that rush of energy. He gradually got back into his normal state and his balanced style.

"Yuzuki, we need something else…actually, somebody else. I cannot handle this alone. There's too much to be done. I have to survey too many things. We cannot go forward without a third person. I will have to watch you during your next plunge. I really can't go forward like this."

"Agreed. Do you have anyone in mind?"

"No, I'm just coming to…I speak faster than I think, for now."

"What should this third person do?"

"Well, monitor the system, make sure there's enough processing power available, switch between the various support applications…that's why I almost lost you. I was at the decoder console, and I lost sight of you for a few minutes, when you pulled that on me…God, I'm still terrified!"

"So you want somebody good with technology…"

"Yes, operating systems, a few applications. You know some—you programmed them."

"I might have an idea…"

Yuri raised his eyebrows, as if saying, *You have a solution for everything.*"

"A student. He's Russian, so you could easily understand each other. He's brilliant and a quick learner, and he's quite open."

"A student...I don't know if that's a good idea."

"Come on, Yuri, be more trusting. Do you feel any reticence for the students you yourself taught?"

"It's not about how good they are; it's about their capacity to discern such subtle...and sensitive things." He stopped abruptly. "By the way, Yuzuki, who did you talk to or exchange thoughts with, during your immersion?"

"I couldn't remember clearly until I read those papers. I was scattered and confused after the experience yesterday. Now, seeing what's written here, I assume that I spoke to Master Takahashi."

"To Moiro?"

"Yes, can't you see?"

She again showed him the papers full of letters and symbols, sometimes senseless, where the word "master" was written a few times.

"Oh yes, but I didn't make the connection."

"It is obvious. Well, my subconscious returns or renders only elements that connect me to my work. Or reasons that make me react about things in my childhood...my mother...the cherry trees in bloom, samurai...in a way, it is normal for me to make such associations. But I do not understand...both my mother's image and the professor's are accompanied by the idea that they speak for somebody else."

"This could also seem normal. Anyone expects to be guided once they cross to the other side. Gods, ghosts… each one with his or her own god."

"I don't know, but I'm sure we'll find out. Back to work!"

They went back to Yuri's office. Yuzuki ordered some sushi, and they ate ravenously. Yuri also drank a glass of vodka, and they started on their calculus and on fine-tuning. It was a good time to go on. Holidays started in a few weeks. The campus would be mostly empty of students, and the teachers around would be even fewer.

The perfect time!

Recruitment

Andrey was stunned.

"I wouldn't have thought this possible!"

"We weren't sure at the beginning either. As I was saying, the success of the experiment is partial. I almost stayed back with the angels. But we are on the right track. I would be happy to have you there…I'd feel safe…"

"I would come, honestly…but that guy sort of frightens me."

"Don't tell me you believe in those stories too…"

"Not necessarily, but Kolotov has a reputation. I don't feel at ease knowing that somebody can scan my brain any time he has the opportunity."

"Andrey, Yuri is an exceptional psychologist. Yes, he can 'read' fears and feelings just by looking at you, because he knows a lot of things about body language and word meanings. He reads the signs on the surface, not on the inside."

Yuzuki stopped for a while to let Andrey digest the information and get some psychological comfort. "I have advanced training in psychology too, if we are to talk about things we don't understand or that seem to be superpowers. But you are not afraid of me, are you?"

"It's not the same!"

"Andrey, I've just told you that Yuri created a mind-reading machine…if he had been able to do that kind of reading with his own mind, why would he have worked so hard to build it?"

"Because he is diabolical…he probably wants a backup plan…"

Yuzuki gave a deep sigh. She closed her eyes, simulating failure. "Yuri was right. You are not mature enough. He warned me that it could be a burden too heavy for people like you. I'm afraid he was right. Again…"

"Did he say that?"

"Yes. He does not think that a student can have a passion for bold and enduring things, built patiently…as I said, he is a connoisseur when it comes to people. And he was right: you are afraid. You don't know exactly why, but you are…"

Yuzuki took a break, watching the pavement of the alley intently. "Good luck with your trip, Andrey."

Then she turned around and made to leave. But before she had taken ten steps, she heard Andrey's voice. "Yuzuki-San…I'll think about it. If you trust him, then I will, too."

"Andrey, you know I have encouraged you to go on the way chosen by your heart. What Yuri or I think must not matter. If your intuition tells you that you must not be part of this journey, then don't! Anyway, this is a difficult, uncertain, risky project. We mustn't go this way if we are in doubt."

"I am not in doubt. I find the project fascinating. I had no idea Professor Kolotov was interested in something like that. We all make mistakes."

"All right. Let me know when you've reached a conclusion. Think well; there's a lot unknown as yet, and don't forget that, up to a point, the project is discreet. And so it could stay until the end, especially if we get no results."

They parted. Yuzuki felt that the technique of reverse psychology would bear fruit. And the same night, she received a message from Andrey:

"I have decided. I'm waiting for your cue. Andrey"

She forwarded the message to Yuri:

"We've got an apprentice. ☺ Y."

Andrey was respectful and discreet on his first meeting with the professor he had so obviously avoided before. Yuri scanned him from top to bottom, even more skeptical.

"I don't remember you. Did you attend my course?"

"No, I transferred to Lomonosov in my third year."

"I see. You had connections."

Then the training began. Andrey was a hard worker and tried to keep pace with Yuri, vodka included. Sometimes Yuzuki joined in; she had forgotten her promise about alcohol. Working with the two Russians, she went with the flow and found an evening glass welcoming—to bring sleep faster. Sleep had become the most important issue for her and for the project. Soon, Andrey left behind his "Evil Yuri" complex and felt enough at ease to discuss with the professor on equal terms—and even to contradict him.

"Gentlemen, is everything all right?"

"No, not really. Andrey's got an idea…he wants us to change the portal."

"Not change it; expand the initial idea," the young man explained.

"Explain." Yuzuki tried to settle the dispute.

Yuri raised his eyebrows to Andrey as if urging him, *"Come on, give us your gem."*

Andrey stood up as he would at an exam. "Professor Kolotov's machine, the whole portal…is wonderful."

"What would I do without your endorsement?" Yuri mocked.

Andrey didn't seem to care. "Now…your initial premises assumed that Yuzuki-San's mind should act as a mailbox, right?"

"Right," Yuzuki agreed.

"My suggestion is that it transform communication into a sort of…chat."

"Magnificent," exulted Yuzuki. Can it be done?"

"Yuzuki, we speak about days of programming, of retesting the application." Yuri tried to reduce her enthusiasm.

Andrey cut in. "The mail program doesn't need to be tested again; we must only update the communication sequence. We can change the communication medium with a compatible one, based on instantaneous communication, or almost instantaneous."

Yuri moved further, like in a cheese game. "We cannot take that risk now. Not now, when we've already gone so far."

"We could save time," Andrey went on decidedly.

"Time is not of the essence in all this experience. The goal here is the finality of communication, not its speed. Besides, I imagined, as did Yuzuki as she fully contributed to the dictionary, the translation routine is from brainwave to words and not the other way round."

"But, professor, now we already have the thought-word pairs…it's easy to match them backward."

Andrey seemed like he was thinking aloud, while Yuri seemed to lose patience:

"We send the messages to Yuzuki's mind in preset patterns, not spontaneously, as a dialogue. We can't simply chat to her subconscious."

Andrey lowered his voice a little and resumed his arguments:

"As I read in the first transcript that was a dialogue. Think of Yuzuki-San's mind as a communication node, which accumulates information up to a point and then directs it to her subconscious; do not build a rapport with her mind as a source. Anyway, it is clear that even there, the dialogue is spontaneous. Can you see…here…Yuzuki-San's reactions? They are not programmed. Why shouldn't we use her mind as an open frequency communication channel? Her consciousness may intervene, and in theory we might too, from the outside, at the same time!"

"In theory we might too? Are you willing to bet her life for a…cerebral teleconference?"

"The initial testing was also theoretical, up to a point, professor…"

"I've been working on this project for ten years! I will not permit you to scorn such a long period of research, Andrey! I've had results…look here, dialogue with the subconscious! We no longer talk hypotheses here. We have results. Get this into your head!"

They were both jostling in front of the screens, displaying results and charts, each trying to prove himself right.

For the first time, Yuzuki felt a fantastically persuasive force in Yuri's voice. His gentle tone had turned into a typhoon. But Andrey couldn't care less about the energy in the voice of the professor. He was in full control of that dialogue, and he showed that Yuri's intellectual superiority did not give him any complex. On the contrary, Yuri was the first to lose it, and he began tearing up some papers in anger. He was mumbling something in Russian.

"Gentlemen…we are tired," Yuzuki said. "I suggest we continue as soon as we are ready with this and, in parallel, that Andrey should develop the instant communication routine."

"I have already developed the first version. It only needs to be tested," Andrey said. "We can practically install both communication solutions in parallel, and we could switch to yours if mine doesn't work."

"Youngman, this is her life we are talking about and her chance of returning from these immersions with her mind in one piece. This is no facebook chat…"

"Yuri, let him install them in parallel. We'll go on," and she turned to Andrey, "with the initial version until we stabilize yours, OK?"

They both agreed. Moreover, around noon, Andrey apologized. In turn, Yuri answered, "Show me how this gizmo works and how you want to switch."

Night found them working and building alternative scenarios. Things were going to be far smoother this time.

They all believed it.

Almost Ready

That day, Yuzuki went back to her apartment early. She was overwhelmed with emotion and impatience for the next test. She noticed Orrin's response to her last message, but she decided not to open it. She fell asleep easily, thinking of what was waiting for her. Her last thought went to Orrin, though.

Orrin...my new obsession!

The next morning, she woke thinking of her Salmon. She had neglected them lately and felt some kind of remorse, the same that one might feel for a pet. At the end of the day, they were what one might call intelligence, artificial, and yet...they were her children and, in a way, her extension into the virtual world.

They had done their job on the given assignment. She read awhile about the basic benefits of genetic engineering, about somatic processes, about the *spindle*[9] mechanism, and about advanced therapeutic cloning programs. She scanned the key words and noticed, under the heading

---

[9] Wikipedia, s.v. "Spindle apparatus", http://en.wikipedia.org/wiki/Spindle_apparatus

"genetic engineering," an article from an online scientific magazine that had been marked as "threat," according to her own classification criteria:

> *"The defense department of the USA has announced that one of their projects is an exoskeleton that will allow marines to run faster and to carry heavier loads. As part of the program, results in the field of genetic engineering are also advanced; a series of transformations is expected with regard to the capacity of the American soldier's organism to turn the surplus of fat into energy in order to resist several days without food. So far, these successful results refer to sleep deprivation—for a period of up to forty hours, during which time the subjects will keep their concentration, reflexes, and judgment unimpaired. The most daring suggestions, however, refer to these organisms' capacity to 'repair' themselves, for instance, to grow a new limb instead of the one lost in battle."*

"By the wind of the Gods[10]…this is taking it too far. Orrin was right; we could get far off the road like this…"

The day ran its course. Yuzuki took a walk in the University park and, on the way home, she stopped at Yuri's office.

He was alone. Andrey had left earlier, having suddenly come down with a migraine.

"How are you getting on?"

"I'm still afraid of that idea of his…and you encouraged the brat…"

---

[10] *Kamikaze*

"Yuri, it can't get worse than the first time. If something goes wrong, we should look elsewhere."

"His idea is not bad, and on paper everything was nicely tuned. But…everything, absolutely everything is based on the fundamentals of the dialogue. For this, I have developed a communication interface, not a common brainwave reader. The essence of this tool is communication."

He looked straight into her eyes. "You've got to promise me something!"

Yuzuki closed her eyes affirmatively.

"You are going to tell him that during the immersion, he is to make no sound. I am the only one who speaks or dictates. He seems to listen to you. Me, he challenges. I used to have more authority before. I'm getting old."

"Yuri…you still have authority. I had to do some work on this kid's brain so he wouldn't be afraid of you any longer. At first he didn't want to work with you; he was scared."

"Really?" One could read a slight hint of satisfaction in Yuri's voice.

"Really. Andrey is just passionate, and as you say, the idea is fantastic. Neither of us had thought of it."

Yuri gave a deep sigh.

"All right, so be it. See you tomorrow?"

"It's Friday tomorrow…yes, in the evening. I want to do some work on my stuff too."

"You're right; you've neglected your work. How's it going?"

"I'll tell you tomorrow."

"OK. One more thing: have you seen a doctor? You know, after…"

"Yes Yuri, of course. I love my work, but I treasure my life. My heart is fine."

"Have a good night!"

"You too, partner!"

Yuri gave her a warm smile, as usual. His friendly look and kind voice had returned.

Yuzuki hurried up. Rain was coming. Her last steps home were accompanied by several large, cold droplets. On the way, she decided to answer Orrin that night. It was a message she would have wanted to avoid. She just couldn't carry so many emotions at the same time. She got her phone and gazed at it for a while.

No, I can't talk to him now…

A short message was better.

"Give me some time. I have things to do. I'm on the last leg with my mentor's project. I promise I'll call you soon. We'll Skype, maybe even next week. I'll answer when I'm done, if everything goes well…
Y."

"PS: My last message was probably a little too emotional. But I was honest, like you asked, and sober this time."

She slept. And she dreamed again.

IV.

It took time to fall asleep, and her soul was filled with emotion. What if she wouldn't be able to stimulate those feelings again? What if her mind was blocked?

But all her fears were scattered away. As though taken away by hand, she rose out of her body. Now her flight toward the world of the archangels seemed terribly real. She felt the summer night breeze and the heavy, cold drops of the rain that had started… God knew when.

She stopped in a huge building, with tall marble columns and granite walls. A new decor. It was a hall whose ceiling she could barely make out. In its midst, in the dim light, sitting on a lonely chair on the checkered floor, a familiar figure was sitting—the master?

She hesitated before talking. Even after his death, she retained the courtesy required by her native culture, whose spirit was so hard for others to understand. The master was looking at her with the shadow of a smile on his lips. He did not make a movement, not a sound. He didn't even blink. She bowed in greeting to him. She summoned her courage.

"I am happy to see you again, Master!"

Her timid voice echoed in the shadowy corners of the hall. As the professor's reaction was late in coming, she decided to press on.

"Master, am I ill with something? All these illusions or images that I don't know how to interpret or how to consider…in fact, I don't understand them."

"We are happy you're back. As you promised and as we have expected, you have kept your mind open."

"I wish I could understand more about you…"

The master seemed to ignore her last sentence. "You called us to our last meeting. We were impressed. We expected a comeback, seeing that we parted so suddenly."

"I did? I managed to summon you?"

"Apparently, yes. We don't know how. But we saw your call. However, you left without saying good-bye."

"I hope I haven't let you down, Master."

"No, I just thought we had lost touch with you completely. Fortunately, we were wrong."

Then the professor's voice sounded like a baritone choir. "We are looking forward to your next call."

She grew confused…somehow she was aware that everything happened beyond reason and wakefulness. It was there, in her dream, in her subconscious, and yet she could make sense of it. Those muddled thoughts made her lose her balance. She felt the big marble and granite hall begin to shake. She felt herself losing contact with the dream space.

But while sliding into nothingness, she managed to shout, "I'll call you!"

She felt the warm sheet underneath and saw the pale moonlight among the clouds. It was still raining—the windowpane was covered in droplets. She opened her eyes for one short second and then fell asleep again. No dreams this time.

Just sleep.

Part Two

DIALOGUES

Imagination is far more important than knowledge.
Albert Einstein

The First Dialogue

Yuzuki had felt her last dream encountering with Professor Takahashi's "ghost" very clearly.

"So, apparently, my subconscious acts like a third part, which invites me to a conversation."

Silence fell in Yuri's laboratory for several seconds. It was a silence laden with enthusiasm as well as with fears.

Yuzuki continued, "Let's start as Yuri proposed, with the 'mailbox.'"

"I feel you've got another idea," said Yuri.

"Yes. I want to write down a number of questions that later on you are to implant into my subconscious via the probe, Yuri. I think that if we create a conscious-subconscious redundancy, we will have the chance to obtain an answer more quickly, which might mean that it would be more accurate."

"OK. What are the questions?"

Andrey sat in front of the console, waiting for his teacher's ideas.

"What is the explanation or the nature of my visions so far: angels, samurai, my mother, professor Takahashi? Who are the people 'at the edge of the orchard' who want to talk to me? Or, well, who are the 'Listeners'? Are they a malfunction or an extrasensory perception I am not aware of?"

They were silent for a while. What if all those questions got no answers?

Yuzuki stirred first and took Yuri's hand, dragging him to the immersion room. It was as though the condemned woman was dragging her executioner, in order to carry out a self-imposed sentence. As usual, Yuri carefully placed the probe on Yuzuki's head. He checked all the connections, started the music, and dimmed the light in the sound-proofed room reserved for their immersions.

Shortly afterward, Yuzuki went into her floating state—unconscious for Yuri, alive for herself. Andrey was waiting in the machine room to send the questions to the depths of her brain. Yuri nodded to him from behind the window separating the two rooms.

ENTER!

Andrey's hand shook for the first time; he had joined a venture that could change his life. Hands to his mouth, he waited for the reactions of the machines he had been rein-ing in like chariots drawn by myriads of horses.

The first curves appeared on the screen. Cursive. Coherent. Constant.

A few minutes later, the waves on the screen stopped. A long break followed. Yuzuki's relaxed face throbbed smoothly. Andrey confirmed to Yuri that he could bring her back to consciousness. This time, the process went smoothly, without incident.

Yuzuki seemed fresh, all her functions intact. "The angels were back. I don't understand it."

"Did you talk to them?" Yuri asked impatiently while taking her pulse and checking her pupils.

"I didn't; I know that for sure. And they seemed to be singing."

They both went back to the computer room. Andrey had already initiated the process of copying, backup, and translation. After a few more minutes, the text editor gave them a few coherent sentences.

"We are the Core. It is difficult for us to explain in a language suited to your understanding. Therefore we shall use a number of analogies which we hope you will understand.

"You have given us so many names and meanings: **MANA,** *Qi, Prana, The Force, the Substance. And in many cases, you have intuited correctly.*

"We, the Core, are a subtle form of energy, difficult to detect with your conscious human senses. Only the very sensitive can sense and feel it, even if they cannot do that in depth.

"We exist as a network where the Flow, the essence of our being, runs continuously. We, as a network, have a collective consciousness, thanks to this constant movement of the Flow, where you intervene by the cycle of life and death.

"The Flow gathers your consciousness and your lifetime experience, and, so we are clear from the start, it is the source of enlivening.

"Your consciousness and your existence are for us, the Core, the matter we feed on. Neither 'matter' nor 'feed' are the exact notions, but we use them to make you understand.

"You have no illness, but you have a gift.

"We would like to know if the language we used is clear to you and if we need to repeat certain ideas or to explain differently what we have told you."

Were they talking to something beyond Yuzuki's consciousness? If this was the case, her mind was only a channel of communication, as Andrey had inferred correctly.

"Are they…God?" asked Yuri rhetorically, gazing at some spot on the lab's ceiling.

"Or an extra…sensory civilization," Yuzuki tried in turn.

"I got scared!" Andrey rose from his chair and began pacing through the room.

"Cool down, Andrey. This must be one of my visions. Let's analyze things…"

"What if we upset them, Yuzuki-san? Maybe they'll… attack us."

"And do what? Invade us? I can well imagine them flowing out of our ears. Please calm down. Yuri, say something, anything!"

The professor seemed deep in thought; his mind was somewhere beyond the events. His eyes were still unfocussed. He raised his eyebrows and said almost in a whisper, "I think we have found God."

"So you believe this is an intelligence beyond my mind?"

"Yes. All the messages they've sent you so far…cherubs, samurai, people you loved…they were just imagined messengers, avatars reconstructed around your day-to-day preferences or around your memories. But they were only avatars. This is a higher power. It's…God!" The professor's laughter was a mixture of euphoria and awe.

"Yuri, we are in a laboratory, three scientists. We are not in church..."

"What do you know about divinity? In fact, what does this crazy humankind know about divinity? I would tackle this differently. Why did they turn up, why now, and why through your mind; and in the end, what do they want? It's strange and exciting, I'll admit it..."

Yuri gazed again at the imaginary spot on the ceiling. "I think that Andrey's idea is really good."

Yuzuki's looked at him blankly then rose her eyebrows, surprised by Yuri's perspective change.

"Let's try a dialogue. The portal is now made of two interconnected gates, the probe in the real world and your subconscious, inside there. These are two communication bridges, exchanging messages, and therefore, I think we could talk to them directly, whoever they are. Their message came extremely quickly. The question is, how long can you resist in there?"

Yuri turned to Yuzuki. "How do you feel?"

"Apparently fine."

"Shall we take another plunge? Although it's more of a launch..."

"Let's do it!" and Yuzuki jumped from the chair.

"Andrey, I need a mike to tell you the messages you need to send to...the Core."

Yuri was still laughing, confused and out of his depth. He had been waiting for such a unique moment for so long that now it seemed he had solved too many things too soon, or at least sooner than he expected. Andrey took the headphones and the spare mike from the installation kit of one of the computers and pulled out a long cable.

"A wireless would've been nice…"

Yuri gave no chance to Andrey's new challenge.

"Maybe not; we already have too many waves…"

Yuri kitted up and focused on hypnosis. Everything went by the book; they were all ready. They didn't fumble as they had during their first attempts: Yuri's technique, Yuzuki's mind-opening, or Andrey's dexterity in handling the applications of the portal.

Yuri spoke clearly. "We understand what you have told us."

Fewer than twenty seconds passed. Then the screen filled again with the words of those beyond Yuzuki's mind. "Before anything else, you must know that you cannot use the Carrier for too long. Its effort is too big. We will let you know when it is time to stop."

Andrey noticed the pattern of the dialogue. If in five seconds, no wave turned up, and therefore no word, that meant that their mysterious interlocutors had ended their communication and it was the humans' turn to speak. If they had anything to say…

Yuri dictated, "Why did you choose to communicate this way?"

"We do not master your language and can only speak through a Carrier. This is the only way we can communicate with you. As a rule, we interact with you whenever we get a signal from an open mind. In the current situation, we have initiated the dialogue with this Carrier because we consider it suitable."

"What is a Carrier?"

"The organism that supports your existence. Your body."

"Do you initiate such dialogues often?"

"This is the third time in our common existence that we have initiated a dialogue. In this incursion, we learned that you are now able to initiate conscious dialogues with us, too. It was somehow predictable, but it is also surprising. We do not fully understand how you did it, but we find the solution ingenious."

Yuri growled with satisfaction. "When did you initiate the first dialogue?"

"The moment you started to evolve toward entities endowed with judgment and reason. The moment when we first visited you was when you started to express yourselves through written signs. We visited several consciousnesses at the same time then. After that incursion, we polished our capacity to understand your language. Since then, we have done that with interest and rigor."

"Why did you initiate the first visit?"

"To understand that manifestation. We realized the capacity of your Carriers to accumulate knowledge and to transmit it down the line in other ways than genetically. We wanted to understand whether that manifestation had been determined by cohabitation with us or by an independent evolutionary leap. We understood then that your evolution is based on a combination of the original genetic basis and the experience of successive generations of Carriers. In turn, this experience determines changes in the genetic structure, as a result of the acquisition of a new evolutionary stage, from one generation to the next. It is a perfect chain you are endowed with but don't understand. It is fascinating for us!"

Yuri was eagerly writing some intermediary conclusions and building clusters of ideas in his head that he wanted to bring up in his conversation with the Core. He had encircled a few key words on which he wanted to dwell longer.

"What do you mean by receiving a signal from an open mind?"

"Imagine that when we relate to you, we perceive a vast expanse of clouds. When a Carrier's mind is open, we get a signal, like a shining, pulsing dot, like lightning."

"What do you understand by an open mind?"

"It's a consciousness that is full of curiosity, which feels the limitation of the space it lives in and feels strong dissatisfaction, restlessness, and yearning. We learned that in such cases, something inside you breaks the limits enforced by your mind and opens communication with us. These minds are not aware of our existence as it really is, but they feel that beyond the limits they have crossed is a space where they can go and where their wishes or their needs can get answers. Sometimes they find these answers; sometimes they don't."

"So, our interaction with you is a continuous process where you intervene in order to inspire open minds..."

"We do not intervene. We remain neutral all the time; we allow that daring consciousness to enter our space. We discreetly guide those thought buds and protect them, because they are vulnerable and confusing. The consciousnesses are like children; they do not realize the power of the Flow, nor do they recognize familiar routines. That is why we have created a landscape suitable to each consciousness, with images or people it knows or loves, to make the journey more familiar. But we do not intervene in either direction—to inhibit or stimulate."

The avatars…

"You create a suitable landscape? Could you explain this idea?"

"We cannot explain. You wouldn't understand."

What do they mean, we wouldn't understand?

Yuri returned to his dialogue with the Core, trying to act up to the moment. It was overwhelming anyway. "Why did you choose Yuzuki?"

A long silence followed. No answer from the other side. Andrey shrugged his shoulders. The Core probably didn't understand the match between the name and the "Carrier."

"Why did you choose this particular Carrier?"

"We have recently received the Flow of another Carrier who lived close to this one. The content of that Flow revealed a few experiences essential to our decision to initiate this incursion. We understood that this Carrier has an open mind, capable of assimilating information in almost any way. We also learned that it has a good understanding of your collectivity, of the way humans communicate and express their feelings."

"Was this enough for you to choose this Carrier?"

Yuri assumed it was Professor Takahashi's consciousness they were talking about. Only he had enough arguments to "recommend" Yuzuki's mind. On the other hand, Yuri wanted to understand how the Core was judging circumstances, and equally, how they were formulating decisions. In the meantime, there came the answer from the Core.

"No, we knew that this Carrier had initiated several incursions into our space. Later we tested its capacity of acknowledging us. We left a few signs in its mind, which it followed and interpreted with ease. It realized in its turn that it was capable of sending us messages, leaving its mind open and transforming its thoughts. Thus we understood that it knows how to make sense of our messages. We knew then that it was the right choice."

Flabbergasted, Yuri looked at Andrey, who was also shocked at what he saw on the screen and heard in the speakers, serving to render the chain of ideas coming from beyond Yuzuki's cerebral "clouds." In fact, this was the interpretation given to the portal by the Core. Somehow, Yuri lived this moment with pride, but also with a certain envy that the Core considered that the dialogue was exclusively the merit of Yuzuki's open mind—even though, up to a point, this was correct.

Finally, the professor broke the silence and asked, "Are you God?"

His heart was racing. Curiosity and fear mingled in his being, which was so close to revelations that humankind had been dreaming about for millennia.

"Part of the things for which your civilization is grateful to divinity are to be found in us. We inspire your existence.

Let's say we are a legion of angels. We could equally be what you call the soul room, although the analogy is not entirely correct. We cohabit with your existence because you are capable of reproduction and evolution. Your perpetuation and your evolution in this conscious form depend in turn on the symbiosis with us. But we are not the creators of the human Carrier nor of its Scheme."

"You do appear as a divine existence, though."

"You probably assimilate us to ideas of divine intervention because you perceive our existence as supernatural. If you could understand it in depth, you wouldn't see it as divine anymore."

For the second time, Yuri felt he had been taken to the *"have faith but do not inquire" area.*

"What should we do to surpass these limits and see things in depth?"

"He who can't see the light can still accept its existence. He can even understand it with his rational mind, but he won't be able to see it. It doesn't mean that something beyond your senses is necessarily divine. There are forms of manifestation you haven't discovered yet. The fact that you don't understand them must not be taken as a limitation. You are in a stage of accumulation, but you must accept that you are still a young civilization."

Yuri felt rebuked. But he got the message, so he soon got over his frustration. Anyway, he didn't have a choice. The Core's parables were quite eloquent. He had to control himself. Suddenly one of his cleansing routines popped into his head.

Patience is a virtue…

"Could we exist without you?"

"Yes, but not the way you are today. Let's put it simply: you would miss the sense of creation. Your judgment would function by other benchmarks, probably in a more animalistic way, if this analogy is convenient, but this would not be the most suggestive model. Do not forget that some animals can create, too. Besides, the Flow inspirits animals as well."

A longer silence followed. Yuri was breathless, fearing that the connection with the Core would be broken before he could ask the question he most wanted to ask.

"And yet, does God exist?"

"You are used to this human-divine duality. The logic of cosmic existence is much more subtle, though. However, the way you interpreted divinity was for us an essential learning point throughout time. You gave a mystic interpretation to all the phenomena you couldn't explain. When you were frightened, you created a ritual. When you did not understand a phenomenon, you attributed it to a God. You went further, and you chose a member of your community to establish and maintain the connection with the divinity—the speaker of the Gods. Then we understood that you were willing to leave your existence and your inner peace to the care of your peers. But we never understood the sacrifice of life in the name of divinity. It is contrary to our way of collective manifestation."

"And why did you tolerate these manifestations?"

"We do not have specific expectations from you. Consequently, we do not judge or correct; we do not dispense punishments or rewards, because we do not construct our existence by hierarchy. We get the Flow back in various degrees of purity. The purer it is, the faster the assimilation."

"We still think that you appreciate a certain conduct on our part as long as we cohabit."

"We appreciate creative consciousnesses because they bring freshness to the Flow. The essence of creation is also beneficial for your future generations who can have a better perspective this way. Still, we learned that, paradoxically, your interest in the generations to come is limited. But we are not the Purgatory where your sinning souls will boil in sulfur and tar over hot fires. And we do not know that such a thing exists beyond us. Judgment is a human creation. The universe does not decry."

"So our existence depends on each of us?"

"Exactly. At the time of your Carriers' deaths, you honor your existence according to your individual choices. The lifelong accumulations of low, harmful energy make the break with life and the Carrier more difficult. Toxic energy also reveals personal choices: possession, crimes, despicable conduct, ill faith. They all weigh really heavily. Equally, you looked up to the sky too often over time, waiting for divine salvation, while the heaven you looked for happened under your very sight, step, touch, or thought. You should have just opened your heart to see it.[11]"

---

[11] Idea adapted after an assumed line in the Gospel of Thomas the Apostle, found in the quoted documentary: "Christianity, the first 1000 years" (video posted by Charlotte Savannah, February 20, 2013) *YouTube.com*

https://www.youtube.com/watch?v=sllaobr9CFk

"We understand that you can differentiate between the various Carriers."

"Yes, some Carriers are more open than others. Some better feel the connection with us, the Core, even if they do not manage to see us clearly; they feel they belong to something beyond their earthly existence. They are those who bring change to your civilization."

"Can you give us examples of Carriers that are aware of your existence?"

"One you call the Redeemer. We call him the Speaker. He had such a life; for us, the Core, he was a positive anomaly. He was born aware of his connection to the Core. We noticed his unique openness and decided to inspire him. And he spoke for us. He passionately exposed his faith, in perfect connection to and inspired by the power of the Flow. He saw the good faith in every single one he met."

"But all his life he spoke about the Father and the Holy Spirit."

"He told the truth. He felt human was a combination between the Source Scheme and the Flow of the Core. He controlled the force of the Flow very well. That was why he could heal, bring back to life, and change convictions; that was why, in the end, he accepted his personal sacrifice. After his death, you understood that you needed a new religion. We believe that his vision was one of holding on to pure faith. After him, many have grasped this lesson correctly, but they gave it different interpretations—mostly limited, according to what they had understood. Or according to what they wanted to sustain further."

Yuri felt that the dialogue was getting into too much detail.

What the heck is the Source Scheme?

He decided to press on with the Redeemer.

"Does this mean, that those who do not believe in the Redeemer have no faith?"

"No, this is a mistake you've been making for thousands of years, and for it, you spilled innocent blood and went to war. The profound faith was defined by all those with great openness to the balance of the universe, regardless of religion. Their teachings converge toward the same destination. The Source is unique. The differences come from the interpretations and the rituals of the temples."

The Source...

"Are we to understand that from your point of view, faith can exist without religion?"

"In principle, this is your choice. You could have a less religious life, but the measure of good faith must be given by creation. Similarly, one can come close to the universal equilibrium following either a religious path or a temple path. Behind faith, there generally is a way of life: commitment, passion, dedication, selflessness—all the things that can make you better and can enrich the Flow. Religion is your rational creation. For us, it was somewhat predictable; starting from your origin, you needed to control and guide the others, somehow regardless of any idea of good or bad. Therefore, for us, it didn't seem such a spectacular creation. Nonetheless, we believe that your religious vocation is beneficial; it is the intelligent manifestation that differentiates you from the other species."

"We may infer, then, that you appreciate religious consciousnesses."

"We embrace the consciousnesses that have faith. We speak here of the faith in universal balance, a connection to one's peers, to nature, or to divinity as you choose to define it. A life lived in creation-oriented faith gives you a much simpler break at the moment of your death. This is what we appreciate. The Flow gathers substance as mankind evolves. The principle underlying the refreshment of the Flow is similar to that of germination: it is cyclical, and it needs a seed, a nourishing support, a substratum, and much care. We, the Core, do not have needs; we simply follow a principle of existence. The base of our existence is what you call a quantum."

"Could you get into specifics?"

"As you yourselves have discovered, the atom is not the tiniest part of matter. In fact, everything is energy. Ubiquitous, it gives us support and surrounds you. It suffices a vibration of this energy's frequency to determine a change of our mutual existence. For instance, your tendency to possess compresses the energy of the Flow so much that the pressure of physical death comes as true purgatory. The break from life, in such cases, is difficult to accept. Feelings like love and selflessness or egocentrism and pragmatism cause certain disturbances in the Flow, which can make the difference at the time of the break. You are inflicting the Last Judgment upon yourselves. The choice of the righteous belongs to you individually, and it starts right from the vibration of the individual feelings and from your capacity to give existence a meaning and to keep the balance of everything around.[12]"

Yuri insisted on one of the points he had encircled in his notes as important: "Can you help us find the right way?"

"We cannot influence collective or individual decisions. We rely on your accumulation of experience according to your free will. At a certain point, your choices are more important than our options. You don't need our apocalypse or our blessing to sanction your occasionally irrational behavior and to show you the right path."

"But could you tell us what this universal equilibrium is?"

"You have found this equilibrium yourselves, several times over. We have kept this writing, which impressed us by its depth: *'Weakness comes after malice and untruth, for what you give, you get; what you sow, you reap; but be aware that the light of your soul and the light of your neighbor's soul come from the same hearth and are left shadow-less. Seek what troubles come from the sources of your neighbor's mind and soul. Bring peace to his soul and clarity to his mind, and your old age will be like a tree with ripe fruit; your bones and your brawn will not fail you, and you will return to the place you came*

---

12 This paragraph is an adaptation after an article read in a magazine during a Bucharest-Zurich flight, in October 2009. I wrote down the ideas as I found them inspiring, but not the author of the name of the magazine. At that moment I had not in mind to write a book and use them in it. Therefore I cannot provide a reference properly.

from, replenished with the warmth of your descendants.[13] All you have to do is embrace this vision in your everyday life."

Yuri kept quiet for a while. He looked again at his notes. For the most part, he had found out what he wanted to know. Then he started again. "Why did you choose to begin an open dialogue with us?"

"We are concerned about a certain manifestation: the Uncarried Flow. It is partly cause for worry and partly for caution. We, the Core, have learned from the cohabitation with you that it is a good thing to receive signals in advance."

"Uncarried Flow?"

Yuri and Andrey looked at each other. As though they had been programmed in advance, both shrugged their shoulders and raised their brows.

"What do you call Uncarried Flow?"

"When a new Carrier is created identical to a preexistent one."

A long silence followed. Yuri had no reply and no questions. The discussion had exhausted him already. A last message appeared on screen.

"We think we must put a stop to this dialogue here. The Carrier needs to recover."

Yuzuki opened her eyes slowly. "He's gone…"

"Yes, Yuzuki, but he'll be back."

"I know."

---

[13] Adaptation after *Zalmoxe learning*; http://www.acumsiaici.ro/2011/legile-lui-zamolxe/

Yuzuki looked around. Yuri stroked her forehead and gave her a glass of water. This time, he had made sure that his colleague's return would be smooth.

"How do you feel?"

"Fine. Very tired this time. I need to sleep."

He let her recover for a few seconds. Then, as curious as a child, Yuri came near her. "How…or rather, what happened?"

"It was like a dream—maybe more intense and demanding."

Andrey was thumping away at the computer. He had monitored the shutdown of the system and had made sure that the whole conversation had been saved.

The portal had archived the first dialogue.

The Second Dialogue

Yuzuki read the journal of the first dialogue carefully. She wrote down a few ideas and tried to make the connection with what she had felt during the immersion.

"This time, Master Takahashi was back. I guess the Core does not run the avatars randomly. It probably adapts to the direction of the conversation."

"Maybe…or maybe it's only the option of your subconscious, based on what you think is going to happen, so, therefore, you somehow 'program' your visions yourself. What do you remember?"

"I was standing in front of the professor. I can't remember too many parts of my discussion with him. I did recognize some paragraphs, but the images are blurred. I only remember the talk about religion and the final part…about cloning."

"Cloning? They didn't mention anything about that…"

"Uncarried Flow…recreation of a Carrier identical to a preexistent one…cloning!"

"You're right, indeed. But equally odd…as far as I know, cloning hasn't happened yet."

"It's not odd…and it's not a hazard. Everything is linked… or seems to become linked."

Still, Yuzuki thought hard for a while. This was a strange coincidence—her talk with Orrin and now the Core's concern. Then she remembered the words of her favorite scientist:[14] *"Coincidence is God's way of staying anonymous."*

Yuri suddenly cut in, "I don't get it. Do you follow genetics issues?"

"Sort of. A good friend does, actually. We had a few talks on this subject during the past months. I also activated the Salmon in this respect, only I didn't have time to look over the preliminary conclusions. I am curious to see whether the Core read this in my mind or had other sources."

Yuzuki was trying to understand why the Core had raised the issue of cloning. She moved back to her talk with her mates. "And apparently, human cloning is a fact. They achieved the first successful human cloning, but only up to a point."

"Oh dear!"

Yuri sat on the nearest chair. Andrey still seemed a little in awe of what was going on.

Yuzuki encouraged him, "Your idea was great, Andrey! Look how much information we've produced in such a short time."

"I don't feel like gloating. Don't you feel somehow unsafe, Yuzuki-San? I don't sleep too well, for fear the Core might steal my consciousness."

"Apparently, they aren't interested in yours," said Yuri. "But yes, I have to admit that we were more efficient using your solution. Good work!"

---

[14] Albert Einstein

"I'll say it again; I don't feel brave at all." And Andrey gave a long, deep sigh. Maybe he sort of regretted he hadn't followed his call and had instead accepted the task of being trapped in this venture.

Yuzuki went into her state of complete intellectual focus, which she hadn't experienced for a long time. "Let's get back to the matter. I think we need a new partner."

"Another one?" asked Yuri.

"My friend ought to be here on my next immersion."

"What friend? And why?"

"The one I was telling you about earlier—the guy with the cloning. He knows the subject as well as we know how neural interfaces work. He has the vocabulary ready and has the concepts clear."

"I can update the vocabulary for conceptual adjustment. Why would we need him? By the way, who is he?"

"An American friend, a former Harvard mate."

She told them about her experience in the States and about her and Orrin's paper. Of course, she never mentioned anything about her still unclear feelings for him. It could be a one-way love. But Yuri didn't miss the details.

"American…"

"Yes. Don't tell me you have a problem with that."

Andrey raised his eyebrows and seemed truly interested in the perspective of a new "partner." But to the contrary, Yuzuki could read only skepticism on Yuri's face, not only because Orrin was American. A new partner sounded like a total intellectual nightmare for Yuri.

"I don't think this is a good idea. I don't think he has the right culture, not to mention his training."

"Try not to begin everything with *no,* Yuri. Don't tell me that the scientist in you cannot get over petty cultural prejudices. You have accepted a woman—Japanese no less—near you. Later, you took on an undergraduate. Why don't you believe an American can be part of this—a professor, a trustworthy person, a professional to the bone, with solid knowledge about our new subject? The Core wants to talk about cloning, and Orrin is the best on that subject. Do you really think that I would jeopardize the project now?"

"We have specialists in genetics, here, at Lomonosov."

"And I trust Orrin."

Yuzuki's reply sounded like an ultimatum, although that hadn't been her intention. But she had beaten Yuri. Now she had to convince Orrin.

It wasn't difficult. Forty-eight hours after he talked to Yuzuki, Orrin was in Moscow, happy to see her and eager to discover the wonderful thing that had happened to his friend. Besides, he felt that, aside from all her projects, his presence would encourage her and maybe would do more than that.

Yuzuki told him about all the shenanigans: the dream, the portal, the first contact, the worries of the Core. At first, Orrin's logic and reason could barely stand the full impact. Then he grew assured that his friend hadn't turned awry. And when he stepped into Yuri's laboratory, he no longer had any doubts; some kind of fear replaced them instead, as he became aware that this was not a practical joke or a story about angels and nothing more.

His real discomfort, though, came from the fact that he was sharing a room with two Russians.

"You must be Yuri…"

"Professor Yuri Kolotov, actually. Delighted."

They gazed at each other like two alpha males. Up to a point, they did fight for primacy; obviously this was not going to be a friendly collaboration.

"I am Andrey. After I talked to Yuzuki-San, I read your blog. I am interested in anthropology, too."

"Yuzuki tells me you are a real talent. I am happy that the young generation in Moscow is open to ideas from across the ocean." Orrin replied sarcastically.

Yuri couldn't help it, returning a line that was equally unsuitable for the moment and situation: all of a sudden, Andrey had become the prototype of the cultural and academic heritage in Moscow. "Here in Russia, we have maintained our authentic intellectual curiosity, despite the wrong Western perception. You probably come from a world where young people find it more difficult to focus. This is not true here at Lomonosov. Our undergraduates are truly the avant-garde of the new generation of researchers."

Andrey cut in, trying to clear the air. "Professor Hammett, Yuzuki-San must have told you about our project."

"You may call me Orrin."

"All right," said Andrey, glancing first at Yuzuki and then at Yuri. "So, Orrin, this is the machine room. Technically, the portal depends on what you see here and on many other resources that are in places even we don't know too well. Maybe only Yuzuki-San…the whole structure that supports the portal is in the cloud. In the adjoining room, behind the window, is the 'cliff.' There, Professor Kolotov and Yuzuki-San go for the immersions."

"That's what you call the chats with 'some-kind-of-God?'"

"We can call them whatever we like. That's where the hypnosis is induced and then everything else happens. I have prepared a set of headphones and a mike for you. You will probably go in with the professor to dictate the messages you want me to send to the Core."

"Can't I have a keyboard in the…immersion room?"

"Yes, you can…Now, this is how we have functioned so far. The professor monitors Yuzuki-San's status and carries out the dialogue itself, and I have to 'talk' to the machines."

"Great. From now on, I will talk to 'some-kind-of-God' directly, without dictating. Professor Kolotov will continue to monitor Yuzuki's status, and you will continue to talk to your machines. Teamwork."

This was the perfect moment for Yuri's fuse to blow. "Professor Hammett, are you an atheist?"

"Agnostic."

"What's the difference?"

"I believe in common sense. I respect nature and its rules. But I'll admit that I like to discover the similarities among different religions. It is my job. I bet I know more about religious dogma than many of those who wipe the floors of churches with their clothes."

"Bets are fine in Vegas. Here, at Lomonosov, we are in the land of science, so watch out!"

"I'm not an ignorant, though…"

"Perfect! It would be wise, in the interest of the project, to respect the superior intelligence we have contacted as well as the rules of this lab. Rules I make. The things we do here are extremely serious. Maybe you don't realize yet what you are in for. You probably know that I was opposed to your joining us. And I am about to find out that I was right. I am certain that, besides us, the Core will also perceive the 'spirits' you work with as useless and fragile. So I will insist you have a serious attitude; you are a professor, after all."

Yuzuki felt the need to intervene; the amount of testosterone in the room had risen far too high. "Andrey, will you please print the journal of the first dialogue for Orrin? He will want to read it in the park, where it's quieter."

Her last words were very loud and clear. She meant them mainly for Orrin. She had anticipated tensions, but it would take a lot of emotional intelligence for things to go on well in that lab and for the project to advance without any obstacles born out of male ego.

The next day, Orrin seemed to have moved on, but not Yuri.

"Professor, if I pushed it too far yesterday, I am sorry."

"Please come to the next room. I have to make something clear, though: this project is the 'cathedral' I have been building for more than fifteen years. I am the person who asks the questions. You will have priority for those questions that have to do with cloning. But I am the moderator of this show. You are, and will remain, only a guest."

"All right, I would like to make sure that we are going in there with free hearts and crystal clear minds, for Yuzuki's sake. I think we both want this."

"You can't imagine how much I want that…"

"Good morning, gentlemen! I am ready." Yuzuki made her first appearance in a floral print dress. Something clicked in the minds of the three men; contrary to the way they were used to seeing her, she could exude lots of femininity and eroticism when she chose.

The silhouettes in the semidarkness of the immersion room increased the feeling of a clandestine journey. Soon the Core's first message blinked onto the screen.

"We can start the dialogue. We hope that after our first conversation, things were all right with the Carrier."

Yuri did not move a muscle, somehow taken by surprise. He gestured to his new cabin mate that he could start the dialogue.

Orrin said, "We would like to pursue the subject of the Uncarried Flow since, at our level of understanding, these experiments have been carried out for the exclusive goal of improving certain advanced medical techniques."

The message of the Core came back immediately. "We perceive a distortion in the Flow that is impossible to mistake. We recognize a stage the Flow has already been in before. We are not wrong, because our existence is sensitive to your reproductive cycle and aware of the essential moments"

During the break that followed, each of them found a better position in his seat. Orrin went on questioning.

"How do you take part in our reproductive cycle?"

"We accompany the whole process of formation of the Carrier every step of the way. As soon as we get the message that an embryo has been formed, a Flow Bud breaks loose and heads toward it. We inspirit it, and we stimulate its evolution. The Flow acts as fuel for it."

"How do you get the message that an embryo has been formed?"

"The Flow of the maternal Carrier knows. It's an event we can't miss. The first development sequence is critical. The cell is fresh and needs a lever effect, which we provide. Through the Flow, we support the cell in its first stage, like a baby who cannot walk yet. The embryo becomes familiar with the presence of the Flow from the moment it gets into contact with the Keepers of the Carrier, and it will be so until the end."

"It would be useful to know what you mean by 'Keepers.'"

"The hereditary characteristics of the Carrier, its ancestral signs."

Andrey whispered into their headphones, *"Could be DNA or chromosomes[15]."*

Both Yuri an Orrin nodded, accepting the explanation. In turn, Orrin whispered, "Piece of cake..."

The Core went on:

"Once the development is initiated, the nucleus of the embryo is flooded with germination fibers and with the Flow. The germination fibers are the nutrient, the Flow is

---

[15] *Wikipedia*, s.v. "Chromosome", http://en.wikipedia.org/wiki/Chromosome

the energy. Together they provide the force necessary for the next stages of development, following the pattern of the Carrier, such as it is preserved in the Keepers."

"Do you keep helping the embryo, or do you retire at a certain point?"

"We never retire. We are talking symbiosis here. We stay until the end. Moreover, we accompany the Carrier beyond birth, throughout its life and up to its death—end-to-end. As the embryo grows, its need of feeding grows, so food must be taken from somewhere close by. The original germination stratum is limited to the first stages of development. The rest is obtained from the mother's Carrier, somewhat similar to the Flow's refreshment laws inside us, inside the Core. The first mechanism to develop in your original Scheme is the circulation one. And the first organ of the Life Blob is the heart."

"What do you call a Life Blob?"

"The baby to come."

Yuri discreetly crossed himself. He raised his eyes to the ceiling, partly shocked, partly enthusiastic. Andrey had buried himself in his chair, dumbfounded, while Orrin continued to ask questions without losing focus. .

"Where does the limitation generated by the Uncarried Flow come from?"

"The germination fibers are for the most part lost when a Carrier is replicated."

Orrin nodded as if all his questions had been answered. But he was far from having understood everything. "But why this concern for the Uncarried Flow?"

"After the death of such a Carrier, we, the Core, receive energy without matter, which alters the texture of the Flow."

"So you can still send the Flow to such a Carrier?"

"Yes, we can, and we do. The Flow follows the normal routine to energize the embryo. But in such cases, the Flow finds too little germination content, as we said before, which does not provide enough substratum for the inspiriting and the subsequent development of both embryo and Flow."

Yuri was still trying to get things clear. Orrin was taking notes. Shortly afterward, he started the dialogue again. "Is a perfect replication of a Carrier possible?"

"Not as far as we understand. But that does not mean it is not possible. We only control the Flow, which follows the contour of what it finds, and not the Scheme behind it. The Scheme encrypted in the Keepers is not our creation."

"Are we to understand, then, that the artificial replication of the Carriers is a threat to the Core?"

"If it is a threat, it is a threat for you."

Orrin asked for permission to press on, and Yuri nodded his assent emphatically.

"Supposing an optimal replication occurs, could the Carrier thus formed relive its previous experience?"

"Definitely not. The initial consciousness does not transfer to the replicated Carrier, even if it has the original Carrier's exact characteristics. We transform the contents of the carried consciousness; we do not put them back into a recreated Carrier or even into a new Carrier. We do not shelve your consciousness. Admitting that an impeccable genetic construction is achieved, the Flow, with our prescience embedded in it, will recognize that particular Carrier—not from the perspective of its previous life, but only as Carrier design pattern. We, the Core, perceive this replication as an anomaly, particularly because it does not ensure the natural circuit of the Flow. All your failed attempts alter its texture, and because the Flow evolves in its turn, the simple recognition of a previous Scheme does not serve in the learning process. It is a sterile recycling process, and useless energy consumption. To put it differently, the Flow backlashes. It's like teaching new tricks to an old dog."

"But if the replicated organism does not keep its previous consciousness, why can't it have a new life?"

"It can, but we find it hard to understand why you would use an artificial method when you have a perfectly natural one; then what would your advantage be, as long as the perceived consciousness is new anyway? The universe chuckles in the presence of the miracle of life, while you strive to transform the creation of life in some sort of magical, alchemical ritual."

The minds of the two professors fell prey again to dilemmas impossible to solve in such a short time. These were things humankind had been pondering for millennia. The Core's message came as a relief: "We suggest that we end this dialogue."

Yuri surveyed the return from hypnosis carefully. Once awake, Yuzuki looked fresher than after the previous dialogue. It had lasted less time, anyway.

"I had the feeling I could hear everything. I really am curious to read the journal."

"You probably learn from one dialogue to the other."

"Yeah, I guess."

Yuzuki looked at Orrin and then turned to Yuri. "How did you two get on while I was away?"

Orrin kept quiet. Yuri said, "Surprisingly well. Congratulations, Professor, for the questions you asked."

"Thank you, and the same to you. Congratulations on everything! You have achieved a wonderful thing...everything I see here. It's fantastic! A masterpiece!"

Andrey spoke to everyone. "Shall we go out for a drink?"

Orrin needed to protect Yuzuki. "Great idea. Only... Yuzuki needs to rest."

"I'm fine. Perhaps a little bit tired, but not more than after a normal working day. I'll join you," she said.

The evening passed well. For the first time, after a long period, they felt like behaving as normal people; a strange brotherhood. But beyond the prejudices of the people around, they were a brotherhood united by a secret that few people on Earth would have been able to share so naturally.

The Third Dialogue

A few days passed. They had decided to give Yuzuki time to breathe. However, the four of them were dying to find out what was left to find. How long could they keep on like this? How long would the Core be willing to answer their questions? A few weeks ago, they wouldn't even have thought that they could find such answers in their lifetimes.

They had to make the most of the openness of the Core. For sure, this was not why they had initiated those dialogues. But the dialogues provided a unique window opening onto a pathway to knowledge and illumination. And the more incredible the knowledge was, the more sense the insights revealed by "the Listeners" seemed to make.

For the next immersion, they had agreed that Orrin would continue to ask questions until all matters related to cloning became clear, if there was still anything unclear. Each of them knew what he had to do.

As usual, the Core spoke first. "We may begin this new dialogue."

"We understand that our role is to refresh the Flow. Your role, as far as we have understood, is to ensure its continuity toward a more pure and developed stage. Beyond this and beyond the clearly different shapes in which we exist, what differentiates us, and what draws us closer?"

"Basically, you have grasped our symbiosis well. The fundamental thing that probably differentiates us is the premise of existence. You raise the issue of individual existence. We, the Core, act as a whole."

"Still, you rely on our individual experiences."

"We embrace individual consciousnesses. But once embraced, they lose their individuality. We keep these experiences that were acquired individually, but not like separate exhibits in a museum; rather, they are absorbed like an encyclopedia that is permanently updated."

"Would that be the only difference?"

"Probably not. Anyway, your call is to create and experiment, while we keep and transform what you accumulate by creating."

"What criteria do you use when you decide to inspirit someone?"

"Inspiriting is a random process, at a pace perfectly synchronized with your reproductive process. We do not choose the embryos to whom we send the Flow. The Core Buds inspirit all Life Blobs, with no favorites and no requirements. But at birth, the Core Bud's prescience gradually dwindles. It won't come back until the end of life, except occasionally and only when an open mind breaks the barriers of conscious experience."

Yuri spoke, a little flustered, as if he might miss the opportunity. He had remembered something that couldn't wait. "Still, you say you leave the communication channel open."

"Yes, but not for a deliberate dialogue. We left a communication gate open so we could have a dialogue like this one. You signal to us through that gate too."

"Does that mean that you know what we feel or think at any moment?"

"No, we learn everything about a Carrier's experience only at the end of its life."

Orrin had the greatest number of unsolved questions from the previous dialogue. Something about the role of the Flow was eluding him.

"Once gone inside the embryo through the Bud, will the Flow suffice until the end of the organism?"

"Yes."

It was a curt and simple answer, unlike the previous detailed ones. So there was probably nothing else to say.

Yuri took over. Somehow, he sensed, the dialogue had turned into an interrogation, where the two professors competed to catch the Core in an off answer.

"And upon our death, how does the Flow go back to its bed?"

"Like rivers flowing into the ocean. When it returns, the Flow dissipated in the whole body comes together at the center of your experience, where all the information acquired throughout life is gathered. There the transformation begins. The Flow reenters our space and adds new information to our collective prescience. And without the Flow, the Carrier begins to disintegrate."

"So the Flow acts like a lever and transportation system."

"Yes, and something more. It can be used as a catalyst for willpower."

"But you said you didn't intervene in our development."

"No, but we do not oppose the Flow's use in this way. It can be shaped and consequently can bring a decisive contribution to character formation. The more often it is used, the more energy it generates. It may be creative energy or the reverse of that. Anyway, we homogenize the Flow so that your next generations might enjoy superior spirituality. Each human uses the power of the Flow in a discretionary way, as it sees fit in the course of its life. We do not set patterns. We do not create a road for a given ending. Each human starts with a load of pure, neutral energy. On the way, you choose to create, transform, or consume. You decide upon your route and destination yourselves."

The Core continued, as if aware of the mental block outside Yuzuki's consciousness.

"We cannot contribute to your diversity as a civilization, because we exist in a homogenous state, with an optimal concentration of energy that is permanently enriched. This controlled entropy is meant to keep us alert at all times."

Yuri jumped. "How can you be homogenous as long as you live in entropy?"

"Everything in this universe tends to go toward equilibrium. We do as well. There are low energy strata that need to be consumed, and there are stable, homogenous strata. We enjoy a spontaneous state of equilibrium. But every time a change occurs, we reach a new state of an internal kind of symmetry. It's like a kaleidoscope, but not perfectly mirrored. But beauty and creative energy do not come from symmetry. For us, it is a simplified way of looking at things. **The Universe does not look at itself in the mirror.**"

"Do you wish to obtain perfect equilibrium?"

Orrin noticed that Yuri's insistence had become obsessive. The answer of the Core seemed to mirror Orrin's thoughts.

"You spend your life looking for perfection and equilibrium instead of allowing the game of asymmetry to accomplish itself. The answer, then, is no; we do not wish to reach perfect equilibrium. For us, it is not relevant."

Orrin tried to change the course of the dialog:

"Could you exist without us?"

"Yes, we can exist without you. There's plenty of Flow to allow us to do so. Anyway, we can convert our energy for different universal purposes. Coexistence with you is not a definitive option for us. We can be in other symbioses at the same time. But do not imagine that we could just remove ourselves and leave you behind, without Flow."

Yuri looked skeptical and was apparently unmoved. "How can the Flow be used by an individual if nobody tells him how?"

"One's self-control can be educated. That has to do with the discipline of life and the ability to stimulate your own intuition. Your maturity is gained from one generation to the next, starting exactly from this lesson you've learned."

"Can intuition be stimulated?"

"Yes. In our understanding, intuition reflects the ability to use the Flow wisely for good insight into the future. Those who have this ability will understand everything in a flash.

Many have failed, but those many failures have served as inspiration and wisdom for those who come next. The consciousness of the Carrier we talk through is a good example."

Orrin looked at Yuzuki—his sleeping beauty. For the first time in his life, he felt he had found what he was looking for.

Yuri continued, "But our whole foundation as a civilization is based on rational research."

"Yes, we know that, and we understand that you rely on cause-effect logics. Rationality and logic have ensured your evolution as a species. But you don't have the exercise of treating reason instinctively. It is of course a discipline of the mind that is difficult to assimilate."

Yuri's laboratory was quiet—both on either side of the table where Yuzuki lay and behind the window separating the two rooms.

And again the Core started: "Your essential theories were formulated initially without a complete demonstrative basis; the demonstration came later, following the theory. But every time, without exception, the idea came as a spontaneous illumination. Many of those who made a difference and who wrote the history of mankind, one way or another, left a very valuable heritage about intuition and vision. And they admitted that there was no logical way to discover the elementary, universal laws, but recognized that the discoveries came only by intuition, connected to feeling and to a certain order that exists behind appearances.[16] Metaphorically, they felt their spirits join the universal

---

[16] Adaptation after Albert Einstein.

current of life.[17] They simply **felt** that they were right; they didn't **know** they were right. All they did was use the Flow."

The human side was still speechless. Nobody was writing; they all just listened.

"Intuition and rational accumulation go hand in hand. They require a disciplined control of the Flow inside the Carrier. The better trained the mind and intuition, the better the quality of the Flow. This means you have to learn to maintain the control of the Bud."

Yuri opened his eyes wide, while Orrin was truly dumbfounded: "The Bud stays inside us?"

"Why, of course. We use the same vehicle to get the Flow back to us."

"Where does it stay?"

"Where it first goes: in your heart. It stays there as long as the Carrier is conscious. It is not for nothing that sometimes they say it is good to 'listen to your heart.' If it makes sense, follow it, listen to it, and feel its beat. At the end, the Bud migrates to where everything you have gathered inside you is stored—emotions, knowledge, memories, feelings, perceptions, and motivation. The center of your existence is the last stop of the Flow inside a carrier. The communication gate we leave open."

Orrin tried his chance:

"The brain…?"

"The Cone. We called it a Bud to maintain the semblance of the shape."

For Yuri, the puzzle started to get shaped.

---

[17] Adaptation after Paulo Coelho.

The pineal gland! So the old beliefs and myths mean something…

The Core spoke again. "We think it's time to end this dialogue."

When Yuzuki woke, they called a meeting to discuss their conclusions. All four were in Yuri's lab, around the table in the machine room.

Yuri began. "So they need our deaths to go on…"

"Yuri, this is the natural law. Now we have discovered that we die for a purpose." Orrin tried to keep a more balanced view.

"But they never die." Yuri continued…

"Because in fact they never live, not like we do." Yuzuki felt she can talk about Core's existence

"They don't have pain, suffering, or loss…"

While Yuri seemed to be looking for the dark side, Orrin sided with the Core. "They are our partners. They support and sustain our existence; they come along, not against us. We too survive through them…it is a damn natural revelation."

Yuri left the table. He looked at the sunset indigo sky through the lab's window; dark clouds had gathered on the horizon. His thoughts weren't lighter either.

Not any longer.

The Fourth Dialogue

Yuri had grown absent and somewhat irritable. Maybe he was just tired. Yuzuki knew that since he had come to Lomonosov, he had had no holidays. Even she had allowed herself some time off, but he had not.

The three people who usually took their places in the immersion room now entered it. Orrin was good-humored. He had started to enjoy the dialogues with the Core. But Yuri was looking down and quiet. His body was tense, and his frowning brow was moist. In between his white-blond eyelashes, the blue of his irises was crisscrossed by thin red threads.

"Yuri, are you all right?" Yuzuki asked.

As though snatched out of a slumber, Yuri started and paraded a healthy attitude. "Yes, I'm fine. Let me know when you are ready."

As usual, Yuzuki floated toward the pleasant lights of the Core. It was like a carousel where matter, temperature, and atmosphere made no sense and had no use. The last two immersions had been almost perfect. She had learned how to find the balance every time and how to contribute to the dialogues with the Core as more than just a simple observer. She had learned how to feel the pulsations of that type of pure and protective energy. It was like floating in a boat on a calm sea where the gentle waves—her thoughts, maybe, or the Core's words or perhaps what Yuri and Orrin were saying—made her feel like levitating in a pleasant roll.

She could hear, if you could call it hearing in that medium, the echoes of her friends' voices in the real world. The Core answered like a sort of gentle current that vaguely altered the cosmologic images she perceived with her imaginary vision, like a multicolored kaleidoscope; the process was reminiscent of the actions of a painter who would wash his brush clean with every exchange of ideas. At a certain point, though, she felt that her "boat" hit a larger wave, and the shock woke her from that balanced mirage, imbued with inspiration and spirituality.

In the world beyond, Yuri had taken over Orrin's keyboard. Concentrating, but still in the same troubled state he'd been in all week, he started writing precipitately. Orrin was surprised at Yuri's haste. They usually waited until the Core signaled. It was the right protocol for their encounters.

"What is your goal? Why did you intervene this time?"

"We wanted to inform you about our worries regarding the Uncarried Flow."

"You never thought that, unlike the case during your second visit, we would be the wrong emissaries?"

"We admitted possible failure. It wouldn't be the first time. As you say, there is no failure—only feedback. The news about our existence may be regarded with skepticism. We are aware that you cannot change the convictions of an entire civilization, albeit a young one, which depends either on palpable scientific arguments or on blind religious faith, a civilization that is materialistic and unaware of the energy supporting it. Simple dialogues will change very little. We do not think you could simply say that you have discovered a different civilization beyond the mind of a Carrier. You would be labeled as fiction designers or as simply crazy. Or others could accuse you of blasphemy. The prejudices that are extant in your human universe surface from your questions: pragmatic, predictable, and technical. Anyway, after this experience, you will alter your personal motivations and your life philosophy. But we had hoped that through this set of dialogues, as you are thus directly inspired, you would try to discern beyond reason and to understand why your intervention in the creation of life is useless, unjustified, and a threat to your own existence."

"But we could always demonstrate that you exist, by initiating a dialogue…"

"You are wrong in that. For a dialogue to exist, we have to answer your call."

Yuri was stuck. The answer was prompt and firm. Andrey had also noticed an atypical curve at the Core's last line and a peak in Yuzuki's brain waves. He whispered to Orrin and Yuri, "Gentlemen, take it easy. Our friends seem a little upset…"

Yuri leaned back a little and settled more comfortably in his chair. Then, covering his microphone, he asked Orrin to fetch him some water. Orrin rose quickly and went out of the immersion room to look for a glass. Andrey helped him while Yuri tiptoed to the door and locked it; now he was alone with Yuzuki. Orrin caught the movement and looked at Andrey, who in turn noticed that he no longer had access to the probe.

"Yuri, what the hell are you doing?"

"You stay with what you know best!"

"Yuri, open the door! You will ruin the dialogue…"

"I know better what I have to do. This project is mine and this girl's. We are the protagonists here. You are just passengers. Do your job, and stop pestering me. I know what I'm doing. I have to focus…"

Orrin kept his eyes glued to Yuzuki's body, while Andrey was trying to break in. He soon realized that Yuri was in full control.

"Cut off his mike and keyboard, Andrey!"

"What's the use? We are stuck, because Yuzuki's reversal is now in his hands…we must act gently!"

"Gently?! He locked us out, and he isolated the system. He locked Yuzuki in there…wherever she is now…and you say we should act gently?"

"I thought you were wiser…"

Yuri ignored them. He knew he had the trumps. He went back into a more moderate dialogue with the Core.

"How do you perceive human intuition?"

Orrin couldn't make sense of his question. It seemed to have no connection to the previous discussion. And it also seemed illogical. He glanced over at Andrey, who grimaced in surprise and despair.

"Intuition is the spontaneous state of inspiration and unveiling of knowledge. At least, this is what we infer from your reactions. Most of the time, it appears as a result of previously accumulated data."

"How do you see it act?"

"It comes instantly, and for a while, it opens the gate to us. The Sacred Cone stirs to life at moments like this. The Flow in you and the Flow in our space cross over for a few seconds, and in those few seconds, the inspired Carrier benefits from all the force of our energy. We do not put forward a revolutionary idea; we only provide the context for the Carrier to research it. The acme of intuition is the moment when your consciousness leaves its Keeper for a few fractions of a second and with the help of the Flow, steps into that illumination corridor."

God damn context...

"Can you send us messages through trance and hypnosis, or is it more comfortable for you to do it only in our states of dreaming and delirium or even when we are comatose?"

"We do not grasp the meaning of this question entirely. In our understanding, all of them —trance, hypnosis, dream—can be useful for our communication. But we do not control them; *you* do. We just keep the gate open— both for inspiration and particularly for an exchange of messages—like now."

Yuri rubbed his forehead in anger. "So you want to use this Carrier to transmit to mankind how important our death is to you?"

Orrin again noticed Yuri's malicious and maybe even poisonous tone. Besides, the communication continued to appear senseless.

"Your death is imminent. It is important precisely because it's imminent. And it has become important for our coexistence for all the reasons we already told you."

"Still, you agree that life after death is possible."

"The Flow goes back to the Carrier with certain preknown sequences and perceptions, but this return is random and occurs only in partial sequences. It never returns with a full recognition of the previous memory. *What the caterpillar calls the end of the world, man calls butterfly,* you say. In this sense, yes, there is life after death. You continue your existence here in a different shape, and you go back to relive a new life experience, in a new Carrier and with a different consciousness. You don't come here as you go to a sanatorium, to be cleansed and then to return all nice and clean to a new life. You just begin another life."

"So you do not admit the idea that humans can be immortal."

"As death is imminent, we do not consider immortality an option. Without the interruption of life, the enriched Flow cannot return to us, to the Core."

"And so you do not accept that human consciousness can exist after the physical death?"

Orrin was desperately gesticulating, trying to stop Yuri. Professor's voice was clearly aggressive, all the more as he was talking to an intelligence they could not really see or understand. All of Yuri's respect for the semidivine character of the Core was gone. For some reason, he was angry with the Core instead.

Andrey was also panicking. The graphs on his screens were running haywire. The speed of Yuri's questions had overheated the system.

"We have just explained that a consciousness continues after death, in a different form and with a different meaning."

"Let me put it differently. Why do we have to die to make you happy...to make you able to filter your flows... to perpetuate your existence.... to keep living using our deaths? Is this what you call symbiosis?"

The Core had no reaction. Instead, Yuzuki's body was contorted in spasms. Orrin looked at Yuri in despair and shouted through the window, "Get her out of there!"

"They didn't answer. I won't get her out until they've answered!"

"Are you mad? This is her life!"

"You don't get it. You have no respect for knowledge... and neither do they. They want all our essence and all our wisdom for their existential whim."

"We'll talk about this later...get Yuzuki out of there!"

"I said *I* am in charge of this mission. Not you, not the Core, *me*. I created this mechanism; *I* will decide when to shut it down."

Andrey broke out, "The system is overloaded. It must be stopped; it's running dry. I'm not getting any waves. The translator is dead. As far as I can see, there is no communication, and apparently I have no more constant brain activity on my monitor."

"I said something, you greenhorn! Learn that you have to listen when a professor is talking to you!"

Perfectly poised, Andrey stood up and talked to Yuri imperatively, putting his hand out to Yuzuki's body, looking the professor straight in the eye, "We are talking about Yuzuki here! If you lose her, you won't be able to finish your project. You know very well that your mind is closed. You are a mental mule. She is the only mind capable and trained to carry on this dialogue. You know how difficult it is to find a clean, natural mind, capable of an exercise like this."

Yuri recoiled in shock. He looked at Andrey, amazed…. how did he know his mind was closed? Orrin was surprised too. But luckily, Andrey had pressed the right button.

Hurriedly, Yuri started looking for the resuscitation protocol. He started reciting it like a prayer. No results.

He started again, and again for nothing.

"Open the door!" Andrey commanded.

Yuri did what he was told without comment. The roles had reversed.

"What did you do the last time?"

Yuri answered, embarrassed and hurried. The professor had become a student again. "Adrenalin, adrenalin shock."

Andrey spoke again. "Last time, she went into cardiac arrest. Now we are talking about very slow brain activity. Adrenalin is useless. What else have you got?"

"Nothing…let's run the protocol again."

Yuri kept reciting, like a priest doing an exorcism. Orrin ignored him. He only had one concern—Yuzuki's recovery. He lifted her head and started whispering in her ear.

Andrey listened closely; the words sounded Japanese:

The cherry blossom
So much like pristine snow they look alive,
May be mistaken for a sign of fallen snow[18]...

Cherry blossoms sparkling far away in the mountains
When dawn came they fell unseen...
Were they snowflakes, I wonder?[19]

Spring, ready to go,
Still lingers
In the last cherry blossoms.[20]

The spring night ended with the cherry blossoms.
How many, how many memories
They bring back to you![21]

Orrin started from the beginning again.

His poems worked. Yuzuki's eyes quivered, and then a powerful spasm shook her. She opened her eyes and grasped Orrin's hand, who shouted madly:

"Can you see me? Can you hear me?"

For long seconds, she did not move. They were all frozen. In the meantime, Orrin had disconnected the probe. His friend was looking up, without moving, without a sound. Orrin burst out, screaming:

"YUZUKI!"

---

[18] Haiku by anonymous poem, adaptation
[19] Haiku by Ton–A, adaptation
[20] Haiku by Yosa Buson, adaptation
[21] Haiku by Matsuo Basho, adaptation

"I can hear you. Don't shout! I'm back. I just need to settle in."

She looked around and saw Yuri, his face a grimacing mask. Andrey stood by him, circumspect.

"It was different this time. I was listening to your conversation. Then the old samurai came back. It sounded like a fight…"

"What happened?"

"They pulled out their swords…they surrounded me, as if they were offering me protection, looking up to the skies. It was terrible, terrible! Then, all of a sudden, they left, and I was suspended in indescribable nothingness. It was like a whirlwind…then something like the blast of an explosion threw me back to you. Somehow I was suspended between two worlds. I was conscious, but I couldn't go any further…"

She stopped and looked at her hands, at her feet. She felt her face, her chest, her abdomen. She rubbed her hands and went on, "And then suddenly, I felt like I was held, lifted, and pushed from behind. I could only see Yuri's shadow. Please tell me what happened."

Orrin couldn't take it any longer. He lunged at Yuri and poured a rain of chaotic blows on him. Andrey stepped in the middle, and with previously unsuspected force, he threw Orrin to the ground, through the door between the rooms. Then he pulled two cables and tied Yuri's hands and feet. Desperate and taken by surprise, the professor screamed like a trapped animal.

And because he couldn't stop screaming, Andrey followed in Orrin's footsteps and hit the professor between the neck and the clavicle. This was much more effective than Orrin's actions: Yuri passed out, as if struck by lightning. Andrey had been on the mark.

Yuzuki was trying to understand. "Andrey, what happened here?"

"There's no time for that. We need to make sure you're OK and stable."

"I'm all right."

"Are you sure?"

"I can speak…I can move…"

Confused, Orrin asked, "How did you come back?"

"I came back alone for a while…I ran towards a beautiful Sunset… through some kind of virgin land"

Orrin was still sitting where Andrey had thrown him.

"I'm sorry I did that to you…I thought it was for the best," said Andrey, giving Orrin a hand.

"Yeah, I got it. Thanks."

"Orrin, Yuzuki-San, you'd better go home and rest. I'll stay with the professor."

Yuzuki was still confused:

"What happened here, people?"

"The professor started arguing with the Core." Orrin answered with his fists pointed to Yuri angrily.

"Arguing with the Core?"

"Yes," Andrey responded back. "Apparently, he wasn't very comfortable with the idea of dying. He also seemed displeased that he had to give his Flow back to the Core. Are you sure you don't want to rest a little?"

Yuzuki laughed. It was a tired sort of laughter, mixed with disdain and tears.

"No, I want to know what happened. I'll wait for him to wake up. I hope the blow wasn't fatal."

"No, it just knocked him out for a while," Andrey reassured her.

"Very well; let's wait, then."

Then Yuzuki threw a long glance at Andrey, who avoided her eyes.

"I'll go and see the damage to the system," he said.

Orrin tried to catch his friend's eyes, as though he was looking at a ghost. Finally, Yuzuki turned her head to him with tears in her eyes.

"You have learned *haiku*..."

"Yes, I wanted to surprise you."

"You did, very nicely. I could hear you."

"I didn't think I'd use it like this."

Yuzuki smiled, tired. "I get it; you just wanted to make peace with me. I felt you. Even there, in that black hole, while I was trying to see the smallest particle of light...you said it all, and it was extraordinary!"

She leaned against his chest. It was all she could do before she burst into tears. For the second time in less than three months, she had been a step away from death. All the science in the world was not worth that.

Death could wait.

Part Three

MEANINGS

To one bent on age, death will come as a release. I feel this quite strongly now, that I have grown old myself and I have come to regard death as an old debt at long last to be discharged.
Albert Einstein

Clandestine

For a few good minutes, Yuri was numb after Andrey's blow. He woke in shock, still agitated. Being tied surprised him even more. From the floor level, he could barely see Yuzuki and Orrin locked in an embrace. He could hear Andrey hammering away on the keyboard in the machine room.

Yuzuki rose and reluctantly came close to the professor, who until only recently had been her mentor as well as a professional and human role model. She knelt in front of him and asked in a whisper, "How have I wronged you?"

Yuri tried to sit up. He could hardly utter a word. His jaws hurt after Orrin's blows. "Oh, God! How could you ever do anything wrong?"

"Yuri, we were all living a fantastic story. We were experiencing the live history of religion and science; we had broken so many barriers together…I don't get it…"

"Yuzuki, you could understand. In fact, only *you* can understand."

Orrin hurried to his side, this time only to help him sit up. "What's your problem, Professor?"

"Can't you think without pointing a problem?", replied Yuri.

He spat out some of the blood in his mouth and cursed in Russian, then continued, his voice faint.

"It's about conviction. A belief that says the minds of certain blessed people can live even after their carcass dies. The Core does not agree, but now I know we can use our intelligence beyond death…ironically, thanks to the Core."

"Yuzuki was not dead…" intervened Orrin.

"The state she was in was pretty much the same thing. Her needs were only the superior ones; she was in direct contact with this intelligence…which was quite selfish otherwise."

"They seemed extremely selfless to me," said Yuzuki.

"Had they been selfless, they would have shared their experience more often, through chosen people like you. They would have helped us become a wiser and more mature civilization. A new race!"

Orrin returned to the sarcasm of their first meeting. "Yuri…my friend, I don't think anybody in his or her right mind would want to survive as a brain in a jar, connected by zillions of wires to computers supposed to maintain 'life,' for the sake of post-mortem creation and the right for humans call themselves a 'superior race.'"

"That's what you say, with your two-bit spirituality. Singularity is the imminent step in science and technology. You should read profile publications sometimes…"

"Don't get smart with me! Right now, you are a pile of blond-haired, red-eyed shit. Be decent and shut your mouth, or I'll shut it for you—for good, you lunatic bastard!"

Yuzuki stopped Orrin. She still had things to clear up.

"But Yuri, make me understand, why did you force them? You saw how extraordinarily powerful they are…and how intelligent!"

"Intelligent, my ass! Sorry! We've gotten used to being afraid, to censoring ourselves whenever an apparently more powerful force turns up. We had to show them we have a new perspective, one they do not take into account. They need a warning, too. They feel that only we need one. They were not able to negotiate. Is that what you call intelligence? Where did they go when I asked them a straight question?"

Orrin spoke, less aggressively, but still excited.

"You were negotiating with the Core? Is this your negotiation skill with a possibly divine existence? For thousands of years, entire generations of philosophers, physicists, chemists, mathematicians, and artists have been looking for a type of balanced, respectful communication with the forces beyond, and you…negotiated? Warned them? Who do you think you are, blondie? You were only a stowaway on a spiritual ship, one of the few consciousnesses capable of and worth a privilege like this…"

Orrin put his hand out to Yuzuki, his "spiritual ship," as though he still wanted to protect her from Yuri, afraid that the man's contagious madness might still hurt her.

The Russian replied as if nothing had happened, "All the truly great things were achieved with a certain dose of conspiratorial spirit and sacrifice. You speak as though all your security and intelligence agencies dance in their ballet shoes and compose chamber music for third world countries."

"I meant a scientific brotherhood, beast! And the brain of a wonderful person. You were willing to fry it, only to carry out your grotesque plan!"

Yuri resumed his arguments as assertively as before. "With or without me, this great dream will be achieved. Do you think this is the only laboratory in the world dealing with this issue? Do you think that in the Far East, they just sit and count rice grains? Or do you feel that Europe is asleep? Not to mention yourselves...have you heard of project Stargate? Orrin...my friend...the whole world wants to conquer this new frontier, and everybody 'conspires.' The human brain is an unknown territory as generous as the whole universe. It is a cosmos in itself, and it is here, two centimeters under my scalp."

The man's bloodshot eyes had lost their former liveliness. His voice was full of hatred.

Yuzuki gazed into his transfigured eyes. "Yuri, I felt there was something wrong with you...I've known it since our first failed attempt. I knew you had chosen the simplest solution, the least risky for your reputation and the most extremely risky for me. Andrey felt there was something fishy about you, too. Orrin didn't like you from the first moment. You were our black swan. Therefore, Orrin's question is justified—what's your problem?"

"You are wrong...I never wanted to hurt you. I couldn't allow anyone else to hurt you, least of all myself..."

"Don't tell me your Christian dogma won't allow you!" Orrin the "agnostic" replied.

"Yuzuki, you are part of my great plan. When I first 'read' your brain, I knew that only you could help me pull this off. Your arrival was a true blessing!"

Andrey, who until then had been sitting quietly before the computer, rose from his chair, holding a piece of paper in his hand. "Unlikely as it may seem, he's telling the truth. He never wanted to hurt you, Yuzuki-San. But professor Kolotov is not exactly what he seems to be… nor is he what many professors and undergraduates suspected. He is not a former employee of the secret militia."

Yuri raised his eyebrows. Did Andrey know the truth?

"Yuri Kolotov is mad…or almost. In his youth, because he could not adapt to the rigor of the Party, of the Communist school, of all the institutions he passed through, Red Army included, he withdrew to the edge of the empire. Yuri was sent as a lab technician to a sanatorium where, by coincidence, he would test mental resistance on people with psychic conditions. In such a big country, with so many unknown or hidden areas, losing sight of somebody, even temporarily, is relatively simple. Once arrived at that sanatorium, he managed to grow out of his technician job, and eventually, he became the head of the clinic. As they say, he became master of his own destiny. And he followed a new calling—teaching."

Andrey glanced at Yuri and continued. "Yuri does have certain talents…but he could not control them, as he couldn't control his own life. He is telepathic, on a minimal level, but still…to become a master in this respect, he needed training. Because he could not adapt, due to his sick brain, he could not pursue the training that would have taken his capacities to a higher level."

Andrey sat on the chair where Yuri usually sat during the dialogues. All four of them were now in the small immersion room. The former brotherhood had turned into a circle of skepticism. Andrey went on, looking at Orrin and Yuzuki and holding the probe sprouting all those multicolored wires.

"After the fall of Communism, people forgot about that clinic. Or, well, didn't pay too much attention to it. But the people there, including Yuri, lived on. And together with other stinking rejects of the *perestroika* and with those who couldn't adapt to either system—Communist or post-Communist—he hatched a…let's call it a 'movement.' A sect, after all, with a pretty harsh discipline. Paradoxically, only in this semi-occult medium did Yuri manage to channel his concentration. Yuzuki-San, I hope you won't be too upset, but the sect is called the 'Mind Light'—just like the seminar you work on and train us by."

Yuzuki smiled a sad smile. "He's a schizophrenic," she said.

"Exactly. He has a moderate form, but yes, he's not all up there, in places. He cannot tell the difference between fiction and reality, for certain stretches of his life. He has moments of complete lucidity, like now. He's intelligent, much above average, and probably a genius at times—seeing the portal; but still lost. His type of the illness is not aggressive, however, although the current manifestation might mean that his condition has worsened. So yes, he was right when he said he didn't want to hurt you. He even admires you. Not only as a scientist, though."

Yuzuki grimaced in wonder.

Orrin raise his eyebrows questioningly: how did Andrey find out this?! And when?

Yuri cast a venomous glance at Andrey, who looked away. The student continued however the "indictment" as if Yuri wasn't even there.

"He is obsessed with your personality, with your mind. He's truly in love with your intelligence, if I may say so. As you have understood, his fixation is to keep his brain functional even after death. The goal of the sect he belongs to is not necessarily aggressive, although the sanatorium where he prepared his comeback carried out tests on people with psychiatric or neurologic issues, as I said. Ethically…you'll be the judges of that. They are ultra-orthodox and have rare paranormal talents such as telepathy and kinesthesia…so they have fewer usual mental characteristics. They have raw talents, partly trained but unpolished, and, as you well said, Orrin, clandestine."

Yuzuki looked into Yuri's eyes, which became sharp again, but tired. He was like a defeated, ensnared animal, laid out on the village green.

Orrin tried to figure it out.

"Andrey, how do you know—"

Yuzuki's interrupted Orrin and asked Yuri imperatively:

"Is that true?"

Yuri hardly articulated his voice:

"We only wanted to make an offering to the human mind, by self-awareness. We believe that every individual has the same capacities as we do. Only they don't know how to use them properly. Yes, we wanted to create a new race…"

"...he's a certified lunatic, and we keep talking to him!"

"Orrin...be patient! Please, Yuri, go on," Yuzuki encouraged the professor to move on with his "defense".

"A race where every newborn baby would be perfectly balanced in body, mind, and spirit, where people would be able to use the power of their minds to control their health and emotions and be able to improve their health or even completely heal themselves by controlling their inner and outer energies, without slowly killing their bodies with chemical garbage, toxic and senseless."

He looked at Orrin with hatred. "You merciless capitalists, you are the destroyers of this species. People could do a lot more, yet they can see or feel only as much as you allow them to. We only want to teach people how to concentrate, so they can evolve emotionally and spiritually, so they can make informed decisions regarding what's best for them. This can only come through illumination and self-awareness. Well-being comes from knowing yourself, not from somebody else telling you how to live and how to prioritize your life. We tame the ego that you have overfed and spoiled with the delights of the material life...you and your world of ambition and primacy. *You* have killed the clean, all-knowing spirit."

He looked at the water bottle on the table. Yuzuki understood his need and put it to his mouth.

"Thank you, Yuzuki. The Core is right in its own way. Each of us is part of this magnificent whole. We knew this energy continuum existed, in everything we did, in everything we thought. Everyone's existence depends on this gift, this life promoter; it is a right that each human being should understand."

"And what are you guys doing for that? You sacrifice the minds of those who trust you?"

Orrin's question did not touch Yuri. "No, ignoramus... many of the minds classified as sick are in fact just different. Acquiring this force is taking a gift back through the training of senses, through the stimulation of creative thinking. People need to naturally release their emotions in order to tear apart the systems and the distorted convictions about the world. This is what we do—we give people back their vitality that the Core gives us at birth and that life as it is today inhibits."

Yuzuki was shocked at Yuri's transformation. The earlier "animal" was now a wealth of wisdom, with a fantastic capacity of persuasion and attraction—a light spot.

"Each of us, even you," and he looked at Orrin again, disdainful, "is a wonderful draft of self-regenerative and self-healing organisms. We have this gift from the Core, but we lock it out; we can recognize it only in our physiological processes and in our subconscious thinking. Is that not a great sin, a terrible punishment fallen onto mankind because we have an idiotic education, based on coercion, and because there's no stimulation of the original, creative spirit? We want to return to people what was taken from them, and we want to do that through a structured and sustained process. In this sense, Yuzuki is doing an amazing job...her lecture is one of our forms of training intuitive thinking. She is our outpost..."

"Don't tell me that!" came Yuzuki's desperate reaction. She found it hard to accept that she had been the tool of an obscure conclave.

"Why not? Is it wrong to use the wisdom of the masses and the power of collective thinking and to tell the story in honest truth? Is this not the essence of that holistic approach, meant to help ordinary people read the multiple facets of the reality they have lived in, sometimes altered in the most horrendous and perverse way? Don't they need a directory, too?"

Yuri was using Yuzuki's arguments from their first contact. But Orrin couldn't help rebuking him.

"And you think you can solve all this in one lifetime? No matter how honorably you may present them, this is utopia… and apparently, in order to reach these goals, you go to extremes and make sacrifices." Orrin added to himself, "Idiot."

Yuri continued his plea. "It is definitely a long-term process. This is no easy task…it takes time, patience, and discipline. Again, virtues that you, Yuzuki, have plenty of, through your nature and your nurture. By developing this state of mind, an undergraduate, even an adult, may learn how to perceive what's going on around."

He took a break, seemingly unhappy that he couldn't make himself understood and accepted. "You are judging me because I wanted to be still alive when this project became reality. Isn't that normal? Every architect wants to see his cathedral finished. My goal is to bring this project to life, and we are determined not to give in. Our team was the perfect combination: a large university and an articulate program. Or do you think that I am the lost, lone mule? Do you really think that a project like this can be run by one pilot only?"

He bore into Orrin's eyes again. "I'll ask you again: do you think your government is doing nothing and that it is moral and transparent? Do you think the countless movies, TV reports, and articles are random and that everything that is done on this subject in fiction, cinema, and even in video games, is done only for creative and commercial purposes? Do you think your famous universities have no similar programs? I know, their instruments are different. I…we took it to the next level; we went further than statistical analysis, because we know it is irrelevant from one point forward. But the rush for this new El Dorado—the underside of the human mind—has been on for at least forty years. We probably are the most advanced. Your shitty capitalism has attracted from all over the world only those scientists able to provide a deeply material global platform. You didn't really fight for those with deep spiritual insight…thank God for that!"

He stopped for a while, his blue eyes scrutinizing the void.

"Yes, I know, our work is hard, because it operates with self-imposed material limitations. But it is far more humane! People don't want to think things can be moved by the power of their minds…they cannot see what a wonderful aura those around them have…they cannot accept that by meditation, people can acquire perfect control of their nervous, sensory, and motor systems. They call all of this 'paranormal psychic abilities, occult, mental tricks, and sorcery,' and they cannot get over their own individual complexes and cannot accept that, put together piece by piece, your idea, mine, his…can build a fabulous whole. Like the Core! This journey did this up to a point, until you lost your faith in your inner force. You saw yourselves walking on water, and you got frightened. Clairvoyance is a gift we get at birth and lose later—ironically, through education. Education, as we know, it inhibits certain divine, cosmic gifts for the sake of social, good-citizenship norms."

Orrin interrupted him:

"Do you believe it is legitimate that all people, masses and masses of them, should have extrasensory perceptions? To foresee the future, to communicate with the spirit? Do you believe this would make them better people? Wouldn't that steal away our desire and our capacity to learn?"

"That's exactly the kind of blackout induced by traditional training. *'You don't know anything; I'll teach you. But I'll teach you according to my rules and my methods.'* Orrin, people already have these powers. I wouldn't be a freak in your eyes if you had them too. But because you don't, you are afraid of me, and fear makes us isolated. For your sophisticated ego, fear is expensive."

He turned his eyes to Yuzuki. "Two minds free from any sort of constraint are stronger than two minds fighting with unequal force to survive in the race, for God knows what in the first place. Two open, powerful minds would never have to judge from the angle of wealth, social position, or titles, but only from that of the quality of everybody's life, the true well-being. Sure, there'll always be limitations. Our goal is to bring down, brick by brick, these walls we have been building around us for millennia. Otherwise, we are awesome constructions, probably as awesome as what you saw there, beyond your own mind, Yuzuki. And for that I am happy for you. Few people have the chance to see the truth behind these walls."

"And you knew all this before?" asked Yuzuki.

"I didn't see it so clearly. Now my thoughts are clear. For instance, I knew that the pineal gland—the Cone—communicates with something beyond us, but I never assumed this communication was so well organized; we have always called it the Mind's Eye, and we were right. Only we operated empirically. We never knew that in reality, we controlled the Flow of the Core. We treated those forces as celestial manifestations, as guides, in a somewhat esoteric way, but we did act faithful to God. The only thing I wanted to develop scientifically was the intuition and then the portal. And as God is my witness, I was on the verge of dropping this project when you turned up, Yuzuki. Your presence gave me the stamina to go on, and it was you who helped me get so far. And it would be sad if we stopped here…"

Yuzuki approached him in a more tolerant mood, still interested in Yuri's story.

"Have you made any progress in the training of the intuitive process?"

"Of course, but in the past few years I focused on the portal. I started from the belief that anyone possesses a certain degree of intuition. You only need to know that you do. I was persuaded that, once the portal was finished, it would help me clear up the intuition issue, too."

Yuri postured as a teacher. He looked as if he was in front of his students, except that his hands and feet were literally tied.

"The idea is that this process of intuitive development must be structured. Your lecture is a good pilot. In various areas of interest, you can formulate expectancies based on explicit consequences. As I said, some people will occasionally follow their intuition, when all the other methods they know, demonstrative and factual, do not lead to the desired result. For a long time, people thought that mental abilities stay the same after childhood. But they were wrong…neuro researchers accept today that people's minds are changing all the time and that new connections and neurons develop throughout life. You know better, Yuzuki. We want to use this natural internal characteristic to build a more efficient and, why not, a more powerful brain, at any age."

Yuzuki replied, as if they continued to build scientific hypotheses. "As long as it is not mind manipulation…"

"It's not manipulation. It is a lever-like stimulation. The subconscious is an inert area, an atrophied 'muscle.' Practice is needed, as well as certain training processes in particular areas: memory, attention, and concentration… essential in the real world and totally unused there."

Orrin had lost his patience, the little he had, intervening ironically:

"Professor Kolotov has a master plan… Yuki, what are you doing? You talk to this madman as if nothing happened? And you, Yuri, stop fooling us! You manipulate the minds of those who trust you. You have a big problem if you don't realize this. And if you do, your place is not among normal people. It's like you are raping a patient under anesthesia. You are gone. You belong in the madhouse. Get used to the idea, and stop pestering us with your fancy ideas!"

The Soldier

Yuzuki was speechless. She was tired after her last eventful journey. Even Orrin was assaulted by mixed feelings; he was inclined to say that Yuri was right in many respects, and at the same time, he would have gladly bashed his head in as his madness could have harmed Yuzuki.

Andrey was placid, his face inert, like a robot's. Yuzuki was first to speak.

"Now what?"

"We'll turn him over to the police, of course."

"For what reason, Orrin? He is a respectable scientist, after all. Eccentric, but a scientist. Anyway, from a certain point on, for most people the 'eccentric scientist' is quite normal."

Paradoxically, the answer came from a sarcastic Yuri. He looked at Andrey, who still had the face of a poker player. "Andrey knows best what needs to be done…"

Orrin returned to an earlier question, interrupted by Yuzuki:

"Indeed, Andrey, how did you find out all that? And why didn't you warn us before?"

Yuri continued, "Here's your real two-faced man—Andrey. If that is his real name…"

Yuzuki recoiled. "Andrey? Your name is not Andrey?"

Yuri continued as sarcastically as before. "This is the game we like: who gets whom? You didn't find it suspicious that this 'nobody' managed to control me from behind the window? Or how exact he was when he immobilized and tranquilized me? Few people understand the force behind the 'fist hammer' because few people are practicing *Systema*[22] nowadays. The young 'student' could not control his ego any longer; he has forgotten that it is dangerous to show off with this art. It's understandable; he was concerned to bring me to silence. So…nobody's perfect in this room."

Yuzuki could barely utter the name. "Andrey?!"

"That is not my name, indeed. But it doesn't matter. What's important is that I unraveled the mystery. And I found the traitor—with your help, Yuzuki-San."

"Whose traitor? What kind of people are you?"

"I am the normal one. He is the anomaly." He pointed at Yuri, who was laughing noisily, apparently in a trance, as if his latent condition had advanced rapidly, effacing any trace of lucidity.

"You are a secret agent? A KGB man!"

"That is not my title…and I don't work for the KGB. But I do work undercover."

"But you are so young."

"I am twenty-eight, in fact."

"Twenty-eight? You don't look it. By the wind of Gods, I trusted you so much…"

"…and a good thing you did, too. Believe me, Yuzuki-San, it was a real honor for me to be your student."

Yuzuki took two steps back, as Andrey reached out to her.

---

[22] *Wikipedia*, s.v. "Systema", http://en.wikipedia.org/wiki/Systema

"I do not want to hurt you. I will not endanger you. That's not why I'm here. I just want you to listen to me."

Orrin held Yuzuki in his arms. His eyes said, *"I told you so." And hers, "I'm sorry I didn't believe you."*

"Yuzuki, Orrin, please listen! What we need here is mutual trust. It is a critical moment."

"Damn critical, young man!" said Orrin.

"Things happened maybe a little too fast. Let me explain."

Orrin nodded disinterestedly, simulating self-control, although fear had gradually seeped into his heart, too.

"Yuri has been at Lomonosov for eight years. He joined as a lecturer, apparently coming from nowhere, and he managed to attract people and raise funds for his projects faster than anyone else. Maybe for you, who come from a world where institutions are more solid, this would have been OK, but for us, such a route was suspicious. He's been under surveillance for more than five years. The first signal came by chance: a former Russian professor, who emigrated to America and returned on a two-year exchange program, was the first who 'read' him. Later, we stepped in."

"And who is *we*?" Orrin stressed.

"That is less important. Like you, we have several intelligence services. This is how the world functions." The 'soldier' turned formal. "Listening to Yuri, I almost began to believe him. He has some power of persuasion, doesn't he? And it is not just a teacher's charisma."

"What do the secret services have to do with this?"

"Do you find it a mere gimmick, being able to read people's minds? Not only the thoughts they hide voluntarily, but the involuntary ones?"

He slowly stood up from Yuri's chair. "And that's not the point. After Communism lost its aggressive aspect, there were reminiscences. And there still are, and there will be for a long time. Nothing to do with political doctrines. We evolved alongside the post-Communist anomalies. You cannot allow total freedom to a society that has just come out of a long-term brainwashing process. That madness lasted for almost a century, and the Western world doesn't really understand it. Inertia is great. Well…the idea is that anomalies like Yuri's *'Light'* might exacerbate certain historic deviations that we will only be rid of in decades. Groups like his require permanent efforts from people like me. Similar groups are scattered all over the world. I wish you would believe me. Everything he said is extremely valuable from a scientific point of view, and the principles are uplifting, but we know that nothing in this world is what it seems to be. I am a soldier. It is not my role to refute values and principles. I have the excuse and the privilege of looking into his eyes and saying 'Gotcha!' You, as scientists, have different goals and horizons."

"But in the end, Yuri's story is honorable. I know it sounds silly, but…what is your objective?"

"It's not Yuri. It's those behind him. The sponsors who support him and who have more or less vanished. What you have to understand is that Yuri's 'Mind Light' is only an interface. Yuri is only a pawn. The others are the real danger, because they can use the tools like Yuri's for their own purposes."

"And who are these sponsors?"

"The 'worms.' They are anonymous players, those who can overturn traditional capitalist empires today. They are those who, from time to time, jolt global markets and obscure governments. Sometimes they surface in sports, arts, or sciences, like Yuri's project, but in fact, people like Yuri are their puppets. We cannot just sit on our hands. America finds its outlet in wars overseas and in a fight against a certain type of terrorism. We have our own issues at home. The escalation of the post-Communist 'creatures' is extremely aggressive. Sometimes we are judged as a nation for our 'anti-democratic' reactions. You have no idea how slowly the wounds heal after almost a century of communist experiments. The minds, as Yuri well states, are still closed. The walls, to quote him again, are higher than ever. That's what we are working on."

Yuzuki looked at him with a hatred she hadn't known she could feel.

"Andrey…or whatever your name is…right now, I don't know who is crazier. Compared to you, Yuri looks like a sacrificial lamb."

She stopped for a moment to swallow the knot that was choking her. And the tears flooding her eyes.

"You were my favorite student. What an exquisite actor! The brilliant undergraduate, then the reluctant, fearful one…the good boy, the young erudite…the sabbatical year…all this time you manipulated me to get to Yuri. How naive I was! You lied to me…and I trusted you. Do you realize how I see you now? I only have to find out that Orrin is a CIA agent, and everything is just fine…"

Orrin grinned involuntarily. Then he reacted as if slapped on his head.

"Would you believe a thing like that?"

"I could believe anything...I could believe that as we are speaking, I am mentally manipulated by Andrey... and that everything that's happened so far was only a play staged by Yuri's puppeteers. Or even by Yuri and Andrey together. I could believe that the *Illuminati* are in the next room and that Obama is in fact a failed clone of Martin Luther King...or that my Emperor is in fact an alien. What can I believe now, Orrin? My second mentor is a mad scientist; my apprentice is the Red Square James Bond. You meet dubious people and study controversial topics. And I, I believe everything you tell me, each of you in turn."

"Yuzuki-San, I cannot ask you to believe me from now on. As I said, I am a soldier, and when I accepted this mission, I knew I would hide the truth, that I would hide myself, that I would live in the shadows, maybe even that I would disappoint someone..."

"How can you live with yourself?"

Yuzuki couldn't hold back any more. She needed to scream. And the Core seemed to have given her the necessary energy to make herself heard more loudly than ever before. Andrey stepped back and bent his straight body.

"We each have a goal and a personal motivation. A past, a gray or a black spot. And keeping those in mind, each follows a certain way. Mine...is that of an orphan, deprived of his parents by an idiotic regime. And that ought to be enough."

"And you burn your life and your intelligence in vengeance, hunting anonymous moguls in the corners of a destroyed Communist empire? What kind of goal is that?"

"I see it as putting things right. You should understand the logic of self-sacrifice. You come from a culture where sacrifice used to be honored. Few people understand the affection we have for the spirit of Mother Russia. It transcends political regimes and secret services. You came to love this spirit yourself. You embraced its culture."

"Because I am open-minded, and I live my life honestly. I am free precisely because I have nothing to hide!"

"It's easy to generalize and to say we are all imbeciles and thieves, corrupt hegemons, and crypto-Communists. We live in a reality that is defined differently. We have built our values differently, and we believe in our destiny as much as you believe in *Bushido*, or you," he added, looking at Orrin, "in the story of the American dream, for all they are worth nowadays. Options must be placed in context; that is one of your first lessons, Yuzuki-San, trying to convince us that diversity is good. However, the soldier's mission is to defend his country's borders. With intelligence and dedication…"

"And you are comfortable at the thought that my trust in you is just a large pile of rubble?"

"No, it makes me sad. But I accept it. Otherwise, without this mask, I could have never known you, which, again, I would have regretted. It is better to regret what you did than what you avoided doing."

"Let me tell you something, soldier: you are crazier than that madman. At least he is honest."

She looked at Yuri, with his vague gaze, teary eyes, and desperate, unhealthy smile. Yuzuki went and knelt beside him. She kissed his moist forehead and looked into his sad eyes. For a moment, Yuri was again the kind man he once had been. He smiled a happy beam, like a child seeing his first Christmas presents. Yuzuki understood him. She was indeed special. No wonder *she* was Core's choice... He spoke low, as though for his own ears only, "Thank you!"

Yuzuki turned to Andrey. "Take good care of him. He is pure light, believe me. I can see this now better than either of you."

Andrey stepped away from the door, signaling that they were free to leave. Orrin stopped in front of Yuzuki and looked at Andrey, who kept his eyes glued on Yuri.

"And we can just leave like that, unhindered, as if nothing happened? Nobody is going to ask us anything? The police..."

Andrey wouldn't look at them.

"Whatever you choose," he replied. "As you say, Orrin, what happens in Vegas stays in Vegas. This is not police business, anyway. This is somebody else's business. On the other hand, it is an internal affair; it's got nothing to do with you. You are in Moscow on an exchange program. Which is both true and valid. Nobody will bother you. Why would they? I can guarantee your integrity and your freedom of movement."

"Why would we believe you?"

Andrey gave no answer. He just raised his eyebrows, as trying to say: *"It is your choice."*

"What makes you think we are not agents too?"

"The soldier" smiled slightly ironically. "The question itself proves you innocent. Both you and Yuzuki are clean. We know that. Besides, you were a great help…"

"Especially *me*!"

"Yes, Yuzuki-San, especially you."

Orrin was skeptical:

"You won't say anything about the Core? And Yuri's project…how are you going to explain all the infrastructure, all the recordings…"

"This is not up to me. Yuri's project is valuable. We know it works, thanks to Yuzuki's mind. But the contents are worthless without the subject behind them. About the Core, I don't think anyone will believe me. To whom could I tell this, and what would I say? This wasn't even the goal of my mission. I had to identify Yuri's sources and connections, for his sponsors, the probe, and the portal are only assets in a portfolio. I put a stick in their wheels. Their contact ends today. My mission has been accomplished…successfully, to be cynical."

He stopped for a while. He looked sad. "And then, do you really think the Core will ever start a dialogue again with somebody else? Anybody?"

Yuzuki stood up and asked firmly, "What about my project?"

"It is **your** project…"

Andrey raised his eyes to Yuzuki. He swallowed hard, with his lips slightly parted, while his eyes were searching for a small piece of understanding and forgiveness. Then his eyes darted around the room, resting almost with affection on the computer station where he had lived the experience of his life. It was one of those moments when his soldierly vocation was weakening. He would have dropped it for Yuzuki. But…it was an uncertainty that Yuzuki could now see more clearly than ever. Her meeting with the Core had opened her eyes, all her eyes…seen, unseen, guessed.

Somehow, as recognition creeps into his own gaze, Andrey's shoulders slump for just an instant. Than he took a deep breath, squared his shoulders again, resigned the melancholic smile, and bowed in silence to her, in an awkward imitation of the traditional Japanese formula. And he stayed bowed until Orrin and Yuzuki left the room.

Then they left the lab; and the university; and finally stopped in Yuzuki's room.

For the first time, there were two people in her bed, and it was no longer half-empty or cold.

Echoes...

They took their time before leaving Moscow. They spent a few days packing Yuzuki's critical stuff, mainly her computers and books. Orrin contacted the American Embassy in Moscow, asking for support for their safe passage to California, his home since he had moved to Berkeley.

During those days, Yuzuki was reluctant to leave her room. She had begun to like her bed; she was no longer alone in it. She had read about the "Lomonosov Mystery" on the Internet.

"Police forces, along with the Medical Emergency Service of Moscow, arrived at the Lomonosov University at the Department of Neural Cybernetics led by the famous Yuri Kolotov, who was nowhere to be found.

"The Police found Professor Kolotov's laboratory partly destroyed. Close sources say that Professor Kolotov had had a nervous breakdown and sabotaged his own lab, thus denying the rumors about taking revenge on his former KGB collaborators—since it was suspected that he used to be a member of the KGB. The professor is thought to have fled the country to an unknown destination.

"The university board refused to speculate on the destination of the professor. They wished to impose discretion upon

this subject, out of respect for a 'wonderful colleague and an exceptional scientist.' They declared that they would soon announce their decision regarding the future of the Department of Neural Cybernetics."

Yuzuki read the report and smiled. "Andrey…what an elegant solution. He 'buried' Yuri for good."

"You've got to admit that the kid is one of a kind…"

"What kid? He's my age. Well, almost. Yes, I should have seen it. For a long time, I thought I was guiding his steps and that I was a good trainer for his mind. In fact, he controlled me all the time. Psychologically speaking, he was brilliant."

"You mustn't think about that. You have all your life ahead of you."

"I don't know what to do. I feel I need closure. To go home, for instance."

"Home…?"

"Kanazawa."

"What about me?"

"Come with me."

"What should I do in Kanazawa?"

"What should I do in California…?"

"It's warm in California…"

"It's spectacular in Kanazawa…"

"Let's not talk about this now. Everything in its right time. But a few weeks on a California beach would be good for you", concluded Orrin.

"Honestly, all my life, I have wanted to see the 'museum' of Europe, from one end to the other. To start with the Mediterranean coast. I want to see Rome, Berlin, Paris, London…the North."

"That would take a year at the least."

"What else do I have to do?"

"Your project."

"The Salmon? They are big kids now. They can survive without me. I shall turn them over to the people who need them."

"And all your work? Your PhD? This sudden giving in frightens me!"

"Orry…we are living in an experience studded with perceptions. I have learned how to survive it. I don't know if it's OK. Anyway, its values are temporary. And then, Orry…I was there…"

She looked melancholy when she traced an indefinite space with her finger. "Do you think I need another confirmation? I know what I have to do. I know what I am meant to do, and it's not the Salmon."

"I can accept that. But…am I included in your new plan?"

"I hope so…"

**

They had left Moscow six months before. They had spent a few weeks in California and then flew to Kanazawa. Yuzuki introduced Orrin to her father: *Dad, this is the father of my children.*

Yes, two little hearts were beating in her womb. When she had found out, she remembered her mother's words in the cherry orchard. Had she felt even then that she was going to have several children?

Later, she hired a consultant to find a "parent" for her Salmon. They were well received at several large companies and by several large investors. The Salmon proved a great help wherever the intelligence of the masses could be used fruitfully. In the end, she chose to give them to a Japanese company, out of loyalty and respect for her native country. Anyway, in exchange for the Salmon, the company was going to finance the academic program she had in her mind—or in her heart?

What had happened at Lomonosov had to be continued, one way or another. She felt that somehow she had really ingested Yuri's ideas. She had moments when she felt nostalgic about their time together. Aside from everything else, Yuri's mind was brilliant. And she had learned so much from him. She knew that the theory behind his ideas was solid, even if not the way he had chosen to apply it.

Orrin noticed that Yuzuki sometimes felt the need to go back to her work in Moscow.

"No, Orry, I don't miss Yuri…but all those incursions, their preparations, the immersions…I miss my cherubs, the Core and its warmth, the things that grew clearer from one dialogue to another…"

"Yes, I wish I had spent some more time there, too. That chat was really challenging."

"Andrey's idea…you see, each of us contributed a creative part. I am sorry that we people cannot synchronize our life stories. But yes, I regret that it had to end so suddenly. Did you have other questions for the Core?"

"Ooh, yes! I wanted to know whether they communicate with the Source, too...whatever that is...where they come from. Maybe we could have understood the Big Bang thing... if there are other civilizations with a genetic structure similar to ours..."

"Orry, you saw that even the Core obeys certain rules without questioning them. Certain things must simply be allowed to function. I don't think we could always correctly evaluate the sense of things and the reason for their manifestation or the exact mechanism by which they determine our existence. You see, only a short episode of illumination, like we lived..."

"...mostly you..."

"Well, I think you lived it more intensely and more actively than I did. I was only a vehicle. What I meant is that it leaves you floating in a nostalgic agony, intellectual only up to a point and spiritual henceforth. And it is difficult to go back to your starting point."

"We'll probably never go back there..."

"Yes. The Core was right. This has completely changed my life. Do you know that there are nights when I wake up crying? It's neither sadness nor joy; it's only very intense living and that I don't know I want to live again. And yet, I don't think a revelation like this would benefit the large masses. Many wouldn't know how to use it."

She stopped for a moment and then put on her teacher's mask and questioned Orrin.

"What else could you have found out about the Source? It is evident that it exists. What else about the Core? How could you explain their extrasensory, purely energetic existence? Did you want to know whether they were plasma or gas? How could this help you?"

"Maybe we could have understood…"

Yuzuki didn't allow Orrin to go on with his idea. She felt inclined to side with the Core, to keep it away from the curious intruders:

"Nonsense! I don't think we could have understood or assimilated the information, even had they tried to use thousands of metaphors to explain it to us. And I also think that it is good we don't know all the rules of the universe yet. Rather, when inspiration allows it, it would be better to use our knowledge moderately and gratefully—and most of all, humbly. The fact that today we understand more about the pattern of our lives does not make us smarter than the millions of people who probably have lived the same manifestation unconsciously. And at the end of the day, we know nothing more than at the beginning. Maybe we are a little wiser, even Yuri in his madness, but we don't necessarily have a better knowledge of universal truths."

"Had we established a longer dialogue with them…"

"All their messages were full of comparisons and metaphors, Orry. Had we been able to understand the true nature of the things beyond us and beyond our limited brains, they wouldn't have gone to all that trouble. Or if we had been 'pre-scientist' enough and willing—and this is the key word—willing to accept with our whole being that the basic idea is coexistence, then we would not be having this conversation today, nor would we have unasked questions and regrets or nostalgia. It is so clear that we have limitations, so deeply ingrained in our minds that perceiving them or God from a rational, intellectual angle is simply hilarious. Let us allow religion to meditate and science to discover."

She paused.

"I think it's wiser that way."

Closing the Loop

She had once received an e-mail, unsigned, and she was ready to delete it as spam. But a short part of the message had attracted her attention, as it contained the words, "Divine thoughts." It included a coded link, and the text of the message consisted of only a few simple sentences:

"The connection is secure and encrypted. Once open, it is valid for sixty minutes. The password is the destination of your thoughts. Thanks for everything."

"PS. I 'defected.' I'm taking care of the dolphins in the Indian Ocean. It's a blessing. And…as promised: I took good care of him. He sends you his love"

Andrey…her favorite "student"…had kept his word. He had sent her the link to the recordings of her journeys: the dialogues with the Core. She now had them in her folders. She was tempted to delete them. Then she encrypted them, as she used to do before with older important data, and she hid them in a deep corner of her electronic archive, in clouds.

Were Andrey's collaborators carrying on Yuri's experiment? What about Yuri's "anonymous" pals? Her intuition said that they were.

Such questions still haunted her. But she quickly shook them off and returned to the present. Now she knew that each person was the sum personal choices. Therefore, she had nothing to fear. She had talked to the "listeners."

It was clear that time didn't stop for her to remember. That was why she chose to spend her time in company and not alone. She didn't want to care about tomorrow so much or be afraid of it. She just needed to hold somebody's hand. And she enjoyed a good, long sleep. This made her feel better than searching the virtual world, trying to get the wisdom of the crowd.

One thing she hadn't given up: coffee.

Her eyes were wide open, and everything was clear now. She felt truly free, remembering those warm, multicolored flashes, that floating beyond regrets, in a world of illusions and of consuming perceptions of the earthly world.

But…

How true had they been? Since she had no more dreams like those, she had started to doubt all of those things: her former feelings, the experiences she had dared to have, that voluntary disinhibition of the self, and the story she had believed in and to which she had offered her whole being, in a way that up to a point was involuntarily suicidal.

I was a sort of kamikaze!

Still, she felt she needed to keep her faith and her belief unaltered.

And yet…what if all that experience had only been a whirlwind in her mind? What if the Core didn't really exist? What if all those meetings and visions were only the products of a dual consciousness that she had unwillingly built herself, beyond any rational experience? Maybe they had been the manifestations of her powerful ego, which, in her arrogance, she had built at first as a need to harness the excesses of a human civilization that had decayed in places. She had been dedicated to algorithms connected to human feelings for so long that she could only see them as sources of information. That coincidence between Orrin's interests and the Core's worries regarding human cloning still nagged at her.

Could all this effort have been useless? The risks she had taken…she had been so close to death twice…all of Yuri's career, paranoid as he may have been, could have collapsed because of her simple illusions, otherwise so convincing, so present, and so precise. Had she let the Russians look for that "El Dorado" only because somewhere in her mind, the conviction remained that beyond people, or inside them or around them, was a generous energy, a civilization thousands of times more intelligent?

She laughed at the mere thought of such a possibility. One morning, though, she woke up with a persistent thought. She didn't remember any dreams, but the revelation behind that thought was as certain as the air she breathed.

(Humans' thoughts turn sometimes into acts. Their power comes with the words; the will that does all this derives from within. Your thought is the spark, and as far as we, the Core, understand, this is your most valuable gift.)

Then she had no more doubts.

She would often close her eyes, trying to recall how she'd felt during those times of professional dedication. Then, her eyes still shut, she tried to feel the immersions. But those feelings would never return.

The Core was right—nothing happened twice. Nothing could happen again. It was only a new state of equilibrium—and consequently, a new beginning. And, as with any new beginning, it needed a new opportunity. The belief in this new opportunity was essential.

Nothing troubled her sleep any more. She wondered at times how long she would be able to stand this lifestyle—serene, settled, and untroubled by ambitions or daring goals. When would she find the power to serve a confused humankind again? If she was going to…

She had Orrin now. Orrin was her partner in everything—her life and travel companion. Like Yuzuki, who had given up her Salmon, he gave up his constant fight with the conspiracy of the clones. He knew all efforts were pointless.

They had reached the conclusion that they didn't want to live in only one place. So they decided to move from America to Japan and back and for a while to live in a rural area somewhere in Europe, as Yuzuki hadn't been able to visit all Europe like she had wanted to.

It was from the "guilt" of the "Life Blobs" growing inside her. Now she knew that in there, the Flow was working with her DNA as well as Orrin's, and maybe even with the will of the babies to be, and that all of that gave them the force, the faith, and the wish to become humans.

And that later, the Flow would accompany them to the end of their chosen road, back to the Core.

And everything would begin all over again.

Rebalance...

(The Core had learned the lesson again. It was going to build a new way of refreshing the Flow, and it would be more careful and more strict about its circuit and its purity. After all, this was what it had done for millennia—learned from the past. It had assimilated the need to match the Carriers and to generate more power for the Flow to adjust to the transformations it had met.

Every time, every fact was an opportunity to develop. In the end, it was beneficial for the contents of the Core and for the freshness of the Buds.

The fact that humankind was trying to take over part of the Core's role was a matter for humans to solve. Yes, humankind was still spiritually fragile and still couldn't define its own limits. Therefore, the Core was going to guide its own freshness even more diligently, not only for the Carriers, but also for the Core itself...

...which had managed to contribute to this miraculous construction—human life—throughout the times. In theory, nothing could change the belief in the Core's collective self. It had evolved from one human generation to the other, from one individual experience to the other. That was what it was meant to do, and in that, it would never fail.

Nonetheless…the recent incursion had raised questions that had gotten no answers. Because this miraculous construction, the human being, had another partner…

The Source.

Did it know what humankind dreamed of?
If yes, when would it make itself heard?
And more importantly…how was it going to do that?)

THE END